*"YOU DON'T HAVE
TO ACT THE INNOCENT
ANY LONGER,"*

Alan said in a rough, uneven tone. "From now on we're just two consenting adults. I had a feeling we'd arrive at this point the first time I saw you."

Paige stood rigid in his grasp, trying to ignore the flood of awareness between them. She knew instantly she was beyond her depth—that she was being submerged by waves of feeling so tantalizing that it was painful to resist. . . .

SIGNET Romances by Glenna Finley

A BUSINESS AFFAIR

by

Glenna Finley

To business that we love
we rise betime,
And go to 't with delight.

—Shakespeare

A SIGNET BOOK
NEW AMERICAN LIBRARY
TIMES MIRROR

PUBLISHER'S NOTE

This novel is a work of fiction. Names, characters, places, and incidents are either the product of the author's imagination or are used fictitiously, and any resemblance to actual persons, living or dead, events, or locales is entirely coincidental.

○

SIGNET TRADEMARK REG. U.S. PAT. OFF. AND FOREIGN COUNTRIES
REGISTERED TRADEMARK—MARCA REGISTRADA
HECHO EN CHICAGO, U.S.A.

SIGNET, SIGNET CLASSICS, MENTOR, PLUME, MERIDIAN AND NAL BOOKS are published by The New American Library, Inc., 1633 Broadway, New York, New York 10019

First Printing, March, 1983

1 2 3 4 5 6 7 8 9

PRINTED IN THE UNITED STATES OF AMERICA

For Donald

Chapter One

"No person in her right mind would agree to anything like that," Paige Kendall announced to the woman behind the desk. "I suppose you had a reason, but frankly I can't see why you ever signed a contract in the first place."

Her older sister Janet leaned back in the desk chair to gesture at the small, austere office around them. "Three guesses, and try money for a start. You know what it's like out of season here at the beach. Unfortunately, Seth's appetite can't be put on a hold button until clients come in."

Paige grinned reluctantly, recalling her nine-year-old nephew's approach to anything edible. "He could give lessons to a plague of locusts, even on an off day. All right—so you signed a paper saying that you'd work for this genius, but that doesn't keep you from phoning to explain that your plans have changed. After all, he only wants you to type a

1

manuscript—not the Bill of Rights. And if he has one bit of humanity in his soul, he'll acknowledge that you can't be three weeks late for your own wedding."

"It isn't his fault that I had to change the date," Janet pointed out unhappily.

"Well, let him blame the U.S. Navy or your fiancé if he wants a scapegoat. Poor John didn't know he'd have his orders changed either." Paige directed a wary look at the other's troubled face. "You wouldn't be idiotic enough to postpone the most important thing in your life for some—technicality like this."

Her sister gestured toward the sign on her desk which proclaimed "Brown's Secretarial Service—An approved firm of the Oregon beach." "John would probably understand if I told him what happened. He knows that I want to keep the business going until his tour of duty is over. It's just that I didn't have the nerve to mention this hitch when he phoned last night."

"I can see why," Paige told her drily. "Even the most ardent bridegroom would draw the line at that. I hope you realize that John's a pearl beyond price, Widow Brown. And I think it's great he sent Seth an airplane ticket to the wedding. My nephew must be in the stratosphere over this chance to visit Hawaii."

"He is. I feel guilty after you made the trip out here to stay with him, but I couldn't reach you to say that John's plans had changed."

"Because I decided to drive out instead of flying. It doesn't really matter," Paige said, shrugging.

2

"Are you sure that John's sister on Maui can watch over Seth while you're honeymooning?"

"She insists that she'll never have a better chance to get acquainted with the youngest member of the family." Janet made no attempt to hide her pleasure, and Paige thought how nice it was to see her sister enjoying life once again. After all, it had been six years since Janet's lumberman husband had died tragically in an industrial accident, leaving his widow with an income that barely covered the necessities, plus having to struggle as both mother and father to small Seth. It had seemed a minor miracle when John Forbes, a Navy lieutenant vacationing at the Oregon beach, had stopped in Janet's office to get some documents notarized during his leave. One look at the attractive blue-eyed brunette behind the desk made his proceedings take far longer than necessary. The next day he dropped in again for directions to a restaurant and naturally asked Janet if she'd sample the fare with him. When she regretfully declined, saying her nine-year-old son was expecting her home to fix dinner, she thought that would be the end of the matter. Instead, John appeared on her doorstep an hour later carrying a sack full of cracked crab and a small barrel of cole slaw. He pressed his advantage, saying, "There are hot dogs in there, too. When I was nine, I thought they were the last word in groceries. As a matter of fact, I'm still partial to them."

Janet smiled and opened the door to invite him in. "Seth will probably polish them off plus the cracked crab. You don't know what you're getting into."

"Now that's where you're wrong." John had been

3

serious suddenly. "I have a very good idea. All I have to do is convince the other two people involved."

Apparently he was a past master at his task. Paige, at her public relations job in Denver, learned snippets of the courtship from Janet's letters and wasn't really surprised to get a phone call in mid-February saying that a wedding date had been set. Since she still had some vacation left, Paige offered her services as a baby-sitter for Seth during the honeymoon. Then, as the date approached, Paige had left early to drive her car to the coast. It was an extra precaution, since Janet's station wagon barely made it as far as the grocery when she'd last visited.

It was during the drive west that John's plans had changed, and she'd scarcely greeted her sister before Janet was spelling out her dilemma.

"I was terribly afraid that something had happened to you," she'd told Paige breathlessly. "Why didn't you let me know where you were?"

"Why? I wasn't lost. You just have an advanced case of wedding nerves."

"I know. Isn't it ridiculous? At my age, too."

Paige gave her a quick hug. "Thirty isn't doddering, silly. And widows have palpitations and weak moments just like everybody else. From what you've told me about John, he sounds positively dishy, so make sure that you don't miss the plane."

"But that's just it—I may have to," Janet wailed. "John made reservations for Seth and me on tonight's flight from Portland, but there's so much to tell you. . . ."

"I'm a quick study," Paige said, going around to perch on the end of her sister's paper-strewn desk. "What time does your plane leave?"

"Nine—which means we should check in by eight."

"Plus allowing two and a half hours for driving to the airport."

"But you don't want to drive back to Portland tonight. You just came from there."

Paige gestured airily. "I'll have plenty of time to relax after I put you and Seth on the plane. And you're not to worry about that secretarial contract. I'll smooth over what's-his-name. . . ."

"Alan Bayne," Janet said, looking worried again. "But I know that he's not going to like it one bit."

"It's such a fast shuffle, he'll never know what's happened. Besides, I'm not that bad a secretary."

"You flunked shorthand. . . ."

"This is not the time for home truths, sister mine. I *can* type. And, let's face it, there aren't any other applicants. After a day or two here he'll probably give up writing to spend his time beachcombing. Actually, we're doing Mr. you-know-who a favor."

"Bayne," Janet said, breaking into the diatribe.

"Bayne." Paige grinned mischievously. "As in pain. That's appropriate. Anyway, Mr. Bayne will be in such a hurry to get rid of me after sampling my shorthand that he'll tear up the contract and thank his lucky stars while he's doing it."

"Ummm. That depends. Maybe he isn't so fussy about things like that. Some men look for other assets in their secretaries." Janet surveyed her sister briefly but comprehensively. "I like your new hair style. It shows off those high cheekbones of yours and gives you an elegant profile."

"There's nothing wrong with *your* profile. . . ."

"I didn't say there was," Janet replied drily. "Right now I'm thinking about the impression you're going to make on our client tomorrow. Maybe after he takes one look at your figure and deep blue eyes, he won't care whether you can take shorthand or even find the typewriter."

"You make me sound like the second blonde from the left at the go-go emporium."

"I meant it as a compliment. With measurements like yours, you were out of your mind to take a position in corporate public relations. Think of the money you could have made from that modeling job offer in New York."

"I didn't like the long range prospects. Besides, you're a fine one to talk! It's a wonder John ever found you—hidden away behind a typewriter here."

"I love Cameron Cove. So does Seth. And the great part is that John wants to live here after he's finished with his Navy service, too."

"I'm not surprised. Even the air smells good. That's one thing that doesn't ever change."

Janet's office was near the Coast drive—at least three blocks from the beach itself, but there was a marine aura that lingered over the small business center, and all the town's permanent residents were very much aware that *their* ocean was just over the crest of the hill.

Paige, although she'd lived away from Cameron

Cove for the past few years, retained an affection for the Oregon coast despite efforts to transfer her allegiance to snowy Colorado mountains and rugged scenery. "It seems heavenly to get back," she admitted, thinking aloud. "Every time it's the same."

"Even though it means doing battle with some man who thinks he's hired a perfect secretary for his stay?"

"He'll soon discover that he's got a pig in a poke instead." Paige leaned over and patted the top of Janet's typewriter. "That's all right. If he goes into shock, I may bequeath him to Liza. After he sees her shorthand, he'll think he's died and gone to heaven."

Janet looked dubious. "She's a wonderful friend and a terrific secretary, but be sure and check out Mr. Bayne's personality first. It would be bad enough to have him sue for breaking a contract, but it would be a lot worse if the charge were first degree assault."

"You don't have to worry about that with Liza—she can take care of herself."

Janet shook her head. "It's Mr. Bayne that I'm thinking of. If he did anything to insult her—"

"He'd land in intensive care before he knew what happened. Okay—I promise that I'll maintain the peace. Honestly, if you keep worrying about what *might* happen, John will be taking *you* to an intensive care ward in Hawaii. Just go get packed, silly." She softened her words with an affectionate hug. "We'll put the phone on the answering service for the rest of the day and I'll turn into a dedicated career woman tomorrow."

"Don't forget to tell anyone who calls that I'll be back in a couple of weeks. I'd hate to lose any steady customers."

"Just you wait—I'll even find some new business." Paige snapped her fingers impatiently. "That reminds me. Do we have a current tenant for the annex?"

The "annex" was their family name for the rental cottage that she and Janet had inherited when their parents died. Originally built as a guest house to the main residence, it had become a welcome source of revenue afterward when Janet and Seth had occupied the bigger house. While not large, the annex was tastefully furnished and had a splendid view of the cove and, beyond the spit, of the ocean itself. The only disadvantage was that it was so close to Janet's that tenants had to like small boys and big dogs because at least one of each was usually underfoot.

Janet put her hands up to cool her flushed cheeks. "I must be losing my mind—I thought I'd told you."

"Told me what?"

"That I'd rented the place to Mr. Bayne. He wanted a convenient package deal and was willing to pay for it."

Paige had started to open the office door but stopped on hearing this latest news. "Oh, help! He's not going to be easy to shelve when he's within spitting distance."

Janet looked horrified. "Paige, you wouldn't try to break the contract? You promised—"

"I know, I know." She grinned at her sister disarmingly. "You shouldn't take me literally. I'll be a perfect lady with our tenant—I'll have to if he's paid the rent in advance."

"From the first of the month even though he doesn't arrive until tomorrow."

Paige shrugged as she opened the door. "Clearly more money than sense. Have you switched the phone? Good—let's go get you packed and find Seth. What did you leave him doing?"

"Saying farewell to Turk and packing a jar of peanut butter in his suitcase."

"Hawaiian grocery stores know all about peanut butter."

"That's what I told him, but he wasn't taking any chances."

"What arrangements did you make for Turk? I thought I was going to take care of him, too."

"Well, as long as you weren't going to have Seth to watch over, it seemed foolish to lumber you with an Old English sheepdog, and one of the neighbors on the next block offered to take him. Their son is a pal of Seth's and the dog spends half his time at their place, so it seemed better all around." Janet finished locking the front door of the office and smiled at Paige's disconsolate expression. "I thought you'd be glad for the peace and quiet. If you'd rather, I can change the arrangements."

"No, of course not. Turk will probably be happier and won't miss Seth so much." They walked around to the back of the building where Paige had parked alongside her sister's old car. "I'll follow you home," she told Janet, sneaking a quick glance at her watch.

"We should leave for Portland in about an hour to have time for dinner on the way."

Janet drew an ecstatic breath. "For the first time, I'm really starting to believe it's real—that I'm not dreaming. Ouch!" She drew back as Paige administered a quick pinch. "What's that for?"

"To let you know that it's real, all right. So hurry up, will you. That airplane schedule isn't any dream either and we have a long way to go."

As pleased as Paige was to put Janet and Seth on the plane to Hawaii later that evening, she felt a tremendous letdown when she drove out of the airport and headed for the coast once again. The lonely drive didn't do anything to improve her mood, and by the time she reached Cameron Cove it was almost midnight. Janet's house was dark in its setting of evergreens, and when Paige parked in the carport and got out of the car, she couldn't help contrasting her lonely return with the cheerful confusion and laughter of their departure a few hours earlier. Seth's big sheepdog Turk had bounded up the street for an unscheduled farewell, with his dog-sitters hot on his heels. As a result, Janet and her son had departed with the dog barking and half the neighborhood waving and wishing them well.

Paige was still smiling at the memory as she unlocked the front door and closed it behind her. She stumbled over a rawhide bone in the front hall and sighed as she deposited it in a box of dog toys just inside the utility room. At that moment, it would have been nice to have been accorded Turk's enthusiastic welcome instead of wandering through the quiet rooms like a dispossessed spirit.

She shook her head reprovingly and told herself that she was merely tired; it wasn't surprising considering how many miles she'd driven. Without wasting any more time, she donned a pair of cotton pajamas and got into Janet's comfortable bed as soon as she'd brushed her teeth.

She'd left the draw drapes on the big window wall partially open so she could look out onto the balcony, where moonlight outlined tall rhododendrons at either end. Just beyond, she could see a corner of the annex that the elusive Mr. Bayne was due to occupy tomorrow. Which meant that she'd have to keep her bedroom curtains drawn at night for the rest of her stay. "Damn!" she muttered, thinking about it. She stirred restlessly and tried to push her pillow into a more comfortable position, finally shoving it against the headboard so she could catch the moon's glimmer on the breakers beyond the spit. " 'A braw, bricht, moonlit nicht,' " she quoted absently and tried to remember what it was from. Then her tired mind moved back to the unknown Alan Bayne and she said "Damn!" softly again.

Despite her outward acceptance of Janet's plans, the prospect of coping with an unknown and probably difficult employer didn't improve her mood just then. In all likelihood, she'd have to hire Liza for extra hours once he discovered just what a simpleton of a secretary he'd inherited. "At least I'm cheap," Paige muttered, trying to find something good in the situation. The longer she could keep this Bayne man happy, the more profit Janet's books would show. To say nothing of that much-needed rent check from the annex.

Paige turned restlessly on her pillow to see the face of the digital bedside clock and groaned. If she didn't sleep pretty soon, she'd be lucky to get to Janet's office on time in the morning—let alone trying to give an impression of bright, brisk competency when she was there.

She closed her eyes to see if reciting the alphabet would have the same effect as counting sheep. "A is for Alan, awesome and appalling," she began. "B is for Bayne, beastly and boring. C is for cretins and cowards—which is what I am," she told herself a moment later as her eyes opened again. "Lying here, imagining the worst. If Alan Bayne gives me any trouble, I'll feed him to the seagulls!"

The peace of Cameron Cove finally worked its magic, and by the time her alarm sounded the next morning, one look out onto the bright balcony with the birds chirping in the heavy shrubbery told Paige she was really home. Even though she was too far from the shore to actually hear the breakers, the glimpse of distant surf beckoned her like a Lorelei. She put temptation behind her, but she lingered on the balcony taking deep breaths of the fresh, tangy air until the chimes of Janet's bracket clock called her back into the house. She paused at the linen closet to extract a fresh towel and smiled as her glance lingered on the cheerful living room opening from the central hall. "Living" was the operative word, she decided, approving the long couch upholstered in a brownish tweed which was against the stark white plaster. Opposite was the fireplace wall, with a raised hearth and a mammoth brick chimney rising to meet the waxed tongue-in-groove cedar ceiling. The architect had chosen a cathedral roof design, which extended into the adjoining kitchen with its open breakfast bar. The master bedroom at the other end of the house shared the ocean view with a smaller guest room.

As far as Paige was concerned, the light and airy interior made sense, since weather at the Oregon beach was gray and temperamental for a good part of the year, despite the Visitors' Bureau's claims to the contrary. Even then, her glance toward the window showed that the dew lingering on the rhododendron leaves was a forerunner of things to come. There were clouds massing to the south—a sure sign that a rain squall would be passing through later in the morning.

She dressed accordingly after her shower—a wool challis shirtwaist in a rust-green Indian print that was suitable for the office yet warm enough to combat the drafts. She hesitated over her footwear, knowing that boots would be sensible but finally choosing a pair of pumps that were flattering and could survive a dash through the puddles. She surveyed herself in the full-length bedroom mirror afterward and made a face at her earnest reflection. The collar-length hair style that Janet had admired was easy to take care of, but it gave her a youthful air that she would have traded for more sophistication just then.

She pulled her hair back in an impulsive move and then frowned as she saw the result. Skinned back, the style certainly made her look older, but there was also a distinct resemblance to Liza's "brush it, braid it, and forget it" hairdo.

Janet's part-time helper followed the same offhand approach to most amenities. Raised by an embittered aunt after her mother had died and her father walked away, Liza had been brought up on a litany of the evils of everything masculine and faithfully followed the doctrine even after her aunt died. She generally appeared in tailored blouses and tweed skirts whose only claim to fame was that they'd never wear out. As Janet once said ruefully, "They wouldn't dare. You'd have to drive a stake through the hem before you could haul them to a rummage sale."

At age thirty-two, Liza further proclaimed her independence by living alone in a small house a few blocks from the office. She was unfailingly loyal to Janet and indulged Seth and Turk with equal attention. She was also a highly efficient secretary, and Janet's patrons went away dazed by such a phenomenon—if they didn't mind having their grammar questioned, spelling corrected, and being subjected to sharp verbal abuse. The latter occurred when a male patron occasionally attempted a friendly pat on the shoulder. One had even attempted a pinch on Liza's tweed-covered derriere and was shoved down the front steps for his efforts. Janet, coming back from a coffee break, had seen the man's jacket thrown out after him as he limped to the sidewalk. "Liza told me that he'd changed his mind after he learned our fees," Janet reported to Paige afterward. "She must have felt guilty about losing the account though, because she insisted on painting the inside of the office afterward."

"What happened then?" Paige had asked.

"I was so delighted to get that painting done that I told her she had my permission to push the whole city council off the seawall."

Paige smiled at her reflection in the mirror as she recalled it. Then she brushed her hair again, letting it fall in soft waves to her collar where it flipped up in a casual fashion. Leaning closer, she made sure that her eyebrow pencil hadn't gone astray and slipped a clear red lipstick into her skirt pocket—to be applied after breakfast.

A glance at her watch showed that there was only twelve minutes for cold cereal and fruit if she were going to be at work on time. Fortunately, there was a percolator at the office, or she could put the phone on the recorder in mid-morning and go down the street to a coffee shop and catch up with the local gossip.

Fifteen minutes later she was hurrying out of the house and into her car. As she backed out onto the quiet cul-de-sac, she thought again what a good job the architect had done designing the house for its setting. The weathered rough cedar structure with its hand-split shake roof nestled among the evergreens as if it were native, too. Only the muted color of brick on the mammoth fireplace chimney provided a distinct contrast to the greens and browns of the outdoors. The annex behind embodied the same simplicity of line, which Paige thought made marvelous sense. With the natural glories of the broad beach and the ocean view beyond the spit, who needed anything else?

And how nice that Janet had found someone who admired the same scenery, Paige told herself as she drove toward the office. She pulled up at the highway and turned left, thinking that tomorrow would be the soonest she could expect to hear a firsthand account of the wedding. It would have been nice to have been there in person but hardly practical, considering the distance involved and the state of her bank account if she bought Janet and John the present she had in mind. She'd better be thinking about more practical things—like making sure that she didn't lose any of Janet's steady customers and arranging a schedule with Liza so that the phone would be properly covered during business hours. In fact, she decided, that should be the first thing on the agenda—right after plugging in the coffeepot.

It seemed like old times when she sat down at Janet's desk a little later. By then, the electric percolator was making cheerful noises atop a two-drawer metal file cabinet at her elbow, and the baseboard electric heaters were quickly taking the chill off the room. Paige readied a clean mug for use when the perking finished and reached for the phone to call Liza at home.

Liza picked up her receiver in the middle of the second ring. "You aren't wasting any time," she said, even before Paige could identify herself. "I thought you'd be sleeping in this morning. Did they get off all right?"

Paige grinned at the familiar onslaught delivered in a brisk, no-nonsense tone. "Shall I take that one topic at a time?"

"It's too early for games. Was Janet in tears when she left?"

"Just a little wet at the edges. Seth wouldn't have forgiven us if we'd taken the gloss off his first plane ride."

"You both spoil that boy. . . ."

"Who bought him all those comic books to read on the plane?"

"I thought your sister needed a little peace and quiet during the trip," Liza said, undaunted.

"You should have driven up to Portland with us."

"It was a family time. Have you heard from Mr. Bayne yet?"

"Nary a word so far." Paige turned to pour her coffee, keeping the receiver at her ear with her other hand. "I don't expect him for another two hours at least. If he spent the night in Portland and has to drive down—it'll be a while yet."

"Maybe he's an early riser—like you."

Paige refused to rise to a familiar taunt. It was common knowledge that she was the member of the family who liked to both stay up and get up late if she had a choice. "I'm reforming in my old age," she said easily. "Besides, I can't find a job where you can report at eleven o'clock in the morning."

"You should come back and work in the Cove. It wouldn't be hard for you to find a job—Thor would let you write your own ticket. At least that's what he told Janet."

"Thor's just a friend, so it's better this way." Paige took a careful swallow of coffee and then swung around to rest her shoes on the heater behind her, leaning precariously back against the desk in Janet's swivel chair. "How is Thor's hotel business?"

"I haven't heard too many complaints," Liza replied calmly. Thor Goransen managed the Conquistador—a popular resort hotel just a few miles north of Cameron Cove—and was well known to both of them. His father owned the hotel and had managed it until a crippling auto accident had made him limit his activities a few years before. Thor had taken over and, to no one's surprise, had more than held his own in a very competitive league. "Does he know you're in town yet?" Liza asked. Then, without waiting for an answer, she went on drily, "That's a silly question. You wouldn't be having coffee alone if he did."

Paige almost dropped the mug she was holding. "How did you know I was drinking coffee?"

"That's another silly question. Just because I live in a small town doesn't mean I have a brain to match. You always had coffee at the office when you overslept."

So much for small towns, Paige thought with a rueful grin. Absolutely nothing was sacred and the closets weren't big enough to keep any skeletons hidden. "All right then—drag out your crystal ball and fill me in on this new client of Janet's."

"Alan Bayne? Didn't she tell you anything either?"

"What does that mean?"

"Just that she's kept the file on him out of sight. If it hadn't been for John waiting in Hawaii, I'd have thought this Mr. Bayne had some sort of spell on her."

"That's ridiculous! You know that Janet wouldn't—"

"Don't get all bothered," Liza interrupted calmly. "I just meant that it wasn't like her at all. Being so close-mouthed about a client. She *did* say that he was pretty demanding in his letter." As Paige let out a groan, she went on inexorably. "If he gives you any trouble, I'll back you up."

"With my shorthand, you may have to." Paige bent forward to put her coffee mug on the file cabinet and then tilted her chair back against the desk again, her feet up against the wall. "But maybe he's a tame old tomcat—the kind who writes one page of copy on yellow lined paper every day."

"Don't you even know what kind of a manuscript it is?"

"Not really. Probably one that he's been working on for the last twenty years. Dull as dishwater and rambling all around the block. I just hope that he remembers to bring his rubbers and umbrella so he won't catch pneumonia if he goes walking in his spare time."

"What's wrong with an umbrella? You can be washed away without one on this part of the coast. You've been away too long."

"Don't I know it!" Paige breathed fervently. "That's another reason why I'm not going to let this Mr. Bayne spoil my holiday. If he doesn't toe the line"—she raised one neatly shod foot and surveyed her ankle critically—"I'll . . ." She paused to think of a suitably impressive fate.

"You'll what?"

"Give me time," Paige began, until she suddenly realized that the question was uttered in a deep masculine voice. She held the receiver away from her ear and stared at it, giving a decided jerk when the same voice came again.

"How much longer do you need? Frankly, I'm tired of standing here waiting."

Paige's feet hit the floor with a thud as she swung 'round to see a man standing by the open front door, surveying her with a far-from-friendly expression.

"Good Lord! Who are you?" she asked, startled.

"What is it, Paige? What's happening? Are you all right?" Liza's voice was shrill in the telephone receiver.

Her alarmed tone was loud enough to reach the tall stranger as he moved up to the desk. "You'd better calm her down before she calls out a posse," he said, nodding toward the phone as he settled into Janet's "clients" chair with every evidence of staying for a while.

Paige felt a flicker of unease, although under other circumstances she would have experienced a different reaction. Most any red-blooded woman would, when faced with a tall, dark-haired male in his thirties who was quietly impressive in a charcoal sport coat and flannels. It was the cold, gray-eyed glance and the angle of his rock-hard jaw that made her say to Liza, "Sorry, I have a visitor. Hang on until I'm finished, will you?"

"I don't mean to tell you how to run your business," the man cut in, "but I'd suggest that you call her back. This is apt to take a while—what with getting settled in the house and arranging our work schedule."

A loud "Oh, migawd!" penetrated the still office air. It came from Liza, who evidently hadn't missed the carrying power of his deep voice. Paige wished that she could give vent to her own feelings even more graphically. Instead, she tried to keep her fingers from trembling visibly as she clutched the telephone receiver and said, "I'll call you later, Liza," before hanging up. Only then did she raise her glance to meet the derisive one leveled across the desk. "I suppose that means you're . . ."

"Alan Bayne."

She winced at his announcement, feeling as if she'd suddenly taken a jab in the solar plexus.

How could she have been so wrong, she thought frantically. This man wasn't the age she'd imagined or the dithering woolly figure she'd calmly planned to manage. It only took an instant to see that he wouldn't put up with anything second-rate, especially in the way of a secretary. Her glance dropped, unconsciously giving him a view of thick lashes, as she wondered how to deal with this newest client and still emerge with her head attached to her shoulders.

She took a deep breath and raised her chin, attempting to hide her turmoil as she met his gaze again. "I didn't expect you so early, Mr. Bayne."

"So I gathered. I couldn't help overhearing." He jerked his head toward the doorway.

Paige wished she could succumb to her overwhelming urge and groan aloud. Apparently nothing was sacred. The man must have overheard—what? All those charming descriptions she'd related to Liza moments before.

"*If* you don't mind—" Alan Bayne cut into her woolgathering and got to his feet. "I still have a lot to do today."

Paige stood up as well, and caught her knee on the corner of the swivel chair, snagging her stocking. "Dammit to hell!" she said, not quite under her breath, as she inspected the damage.

"My feelings exactly." Her newly acquired employer had misinterpreted her comment but there was no misinterpreting his. "I didn't have much hope for this setup even in the beginning, but unfortunately it's too late to change plans now. Frankly, I don't understand how you rate such sterling references considering the way you conduct your affairs." His scathing appraisal raked the office furnishings and came to rest on her stricken form. "I'm surprised that you're still in business. Although maybe there's another reason." This time the glance inspected her attractive figure from the top of her head to her shoes, lingering deliberately on the slash neckline of her dress, which transformed the shirtwaist in a way that the manufacturer could only hope for. "I hadn't thought about the obvious answer," Alan Bayne said finally. "Right now, that doesn't do anything to help your cause. But it's early and that was a grim drive from Portland this morning at the crack of dawn. Let's see how the house suits and then I'll make up my mind. You may be able to handle the requirements after all."

"Exactly what kind of writing are you doing, Mr. Bayne?" Her rising indignation made it difficult to get the words out.

He raised thick dark eyebrows and stared back at her, as if surprised that she needed any kind of an explanation. "I thought I made that clear early on. I'm doing some extensive research on sex in the contemporary novel, and I'll certainly need your help."

Chapter Two

Paige wasn't aware that she'd even moved, but the next minute he was beside her, shoring her up with a strong arm as he said, "You're not going to faint, are you? Here—sit in this chair. Put your head down—all the way to your knees, idiot." He reinforced his ultimatum with a firm shove.

"You don't need to—"

"Stop complaining." He cut into her protest ruthlessly. "You're white as a sheet. Did you have any breakfast?"

"I can't see what business that is of yours." By then, the lightheaded feeling had gone and Paige sat upright, irritably brushing away his hand in the process. She could have told him it was his stark announcement that had left her reeling, but she wasn't sure how to go about it. Blast Janet for not giving her the whole story! Surely *she* hadn't planned to do any research along those lines. . . .

"Damned if I can figure you out." Alan Bayne's voice cut into her reverie sharply. "One minute you're giving off sparks, the next you're acting like a zombie after almost going flat on the floor. I'd better call a doctor."

"You do and I'll not be the one flat on the floor," she flared back. "What in the dickens do you mean coming in here and propositioning me?"

He stared at her as if she'd gone off the rails. "Propositioning . . ." he murmured, perplexed, and then his frown smoothed. "Oh, for pete's sake! I just want some research done; I didn't plan on experimenting." He shook his head pityingly. "With your imagination, you should be writing the book."

"I'm sorry. This is all new to me."

"I *did* write to you."

"You wrote to my sister—Janet Brown."

His eyebrows climbed again. "Then who are you?"

"Paige Kendall."

"In that case, I'll wait and discuss my business with Mrs. Brown." He didn't elaborate, but it didn't take a psychic to know that he wasn't wasting any more time with a substitute. And a pretty poor one at that, his scrutiny showed.

The brush-off made Paige's task pure joy. "You'll have a long wait, I'm afraid. Janet's in Hawaii. I put her on a plane last night."

"How long will she be gone?"

"At least two weeks." It was only to preserve her sister's business reputation that she explained, "She's getting married and her fiancé's in the Navy over there. He had a change of duty and they had to move the date."

"So that's why you're here?"

"One reason." Paige's chin was still elevated but she softened her tone. "I also came out to stay with my nephew, but Janet was able to take him with her at the last minute."

"I see." His dispassionate tone fitted his expression. "What about the business side of things?"

"I'm handling that." As she saw his stern mouth start to curve, she added, "Within reason, of course."

"The contract your sister signed was certainly legal and aboveboard. If you're able to uphold her part of the bargain, we shouldn't have any trouble."

"Yes, but I thought you meant typing—and shorthand." The last came out with a guilty gulp. "I don't know about this research bit."

"You can read a book, can't you?"

"I prefer to discuss this sensibly." She held back when he started across the threshold, determined not to go tagging after him like an eager puppy. "My reading ability isn't the thing in question."

"All you have to do is take notes and keep some statistics for me. Do you have the house key?"

The abrupt change of subject left her staring, open-mouthed.

His lips twitched. "Right now, you look like a salmon they had on display at the fish market where I stopped to ask directions."

Her mouth snapped shut and she sent him a smoldering look before striding back to the desk and extracting a key. She started to hand it to him and then

26

changed her mind. "Perhaps I'd better keep this until you inspect the premises. You might not like the accommodations."

He calmly took the key from her fingers. "Your sister sent a picture. Besides, I've given the address and phone number to my associates, so it's a little late for chopping and changing." He gestured ahead of him. "After you."

Paige took her time about switching the phone onto the answering service and getting into her dark green raincoat. Then she picked up her purse and raised her eyebrows as if surprised to find him still in the doorway. "If you can follow my car, it might be easier. I'll try not to lose you."

"Don't worry. I'll struggle along."

"I'm sure you will," she said, matching his sarcasm and wondering how it was possible to carry on two simultaneous but completely different conversations, the audible one having nothing to do with the unspoken dialogue that reflected their true feelings. "Are you parked nearby?"

"In the lot next door." He watched her lock the office and accompanied her to the sidewalk. "I could do with some coffee first. Is there a place nearby that you'd recommend?"

He was carefully avoiding the fact that there was a perfectly good pot of coffee inside the office and both of them knew it. Paige's cheeks flamed again under his bland regard. She didn't often fail in offering hospitality, and she knew that if Janet had been there, the atmosphere would have been quite different. Even so, she was reluctant to go back in the office with him and even more reluctant to suggest that they have coffee at the house. A restaurant would be better, she decided. If there were other people around, they both would have to stay on their best behavior.

The man beside her interrupted her decision-making with an impatient gesture. "Look, I don't know what's bothering you, but I could finish a three-course breakfast by the time it takes you to make up your mind. Just forget the coffee—it isn't that important."

"Oh, no—" she put an apologetic hand on his sleeve and then removed it at his look of surprise. "I was trying to think of a good place to go," she improvised. "We like visitors to see the best of Cameron Cove."

"I only want a cup of coffee."

"You might as well enjoy an ocean view with it. We'll go to the Conquistador." She paused before adding reluctantly, "It makes more sense to take just one car since we come back by here on the way to the house."

He didn't protest, gesturing her toward an unobtrusive two-door, mid-sized car parked at the edge of the lot. When Paige got in, she surveyed the austere interior with a frown, thinking the subdued trappings didn't go with her ideas of a sex novelist or therapist or whatever.

"It's a rental," Alan Bayne said, although she could have sworn he wasn't paying the slightest bit of attention to her, concentrating instead on backing out of the lot and braking at the busy highway. "Which way?"

She rallied with an effort. "North. About a mile or so. You can't miss it."

"Famous last words." He kept his attention on the traffic, but his expression was more relaxed. "You're right this time, though. I think I passed the place on the way to your office."

She nodded, and when he didn't offer any more conversation, she made no attempt to break the silence between them for the drive to Thor's resort.

The Conquistador's original builders had decided that early Spanish explorers gave them an excuse for the big white stucco building with its red-tile roof. After the Goransen family had taken over as owners, Paige had teased Thor about the architecture, saying that he should put a Viking longboat out in the flower beds, if they weren't going to change the name of the place.

Now, seeing the cars in the motel's parking lot, Paige decided that evidently the Goransens didn't have to worry about attracting customers. There was reason to be thankful that the weather was good because the mission-style architecture looked much better in the sunshine. She saw the man beside her glancing at the padded black leather couches and scarlet rugs in the lobby and hastily said, "The coffee shop's on the top floor—the view is better there."

"Anybody would think you worked for the Cameron Cove Chamber of Commerce in your spare time," he said, waiting at the elevator by the reception desk.

"My sister's on the board of directors," Paige replied, "and she takes it seriously. All the residents around here do." She nodded to the clerk behind the desk who looked vaguely familiar and led the way into the elevator when the doors opened. After they had coffee, she'd have to leave a message for Thor, she thought. If business weren't too rushed, she'd invite him to dinner and catch up on all the latest beach happenings.

They were seated in the almost-empty coffee shop at a window table with ocean beach stretching in a spectacular panorama to either side before Alan Bayne spoke again. "If you're so crazy about this part of the world, I'm surprised that you ever left."

"Even with a shiny new college degree, the job possibilities around here are limited. I was eager to tilt at windmills and climb some corporate ladders after graduation." She waited until the waitress had served their coffee and left before she added, "I'm not looking for any more ladders now."

"Didn't your sister feel the same urge?"

"Perhaps—after her husband was killed. Except she had her son to consider by then, and this is a wonderful spot to bring up a growing boy. Later, she found she had a flair for running a secretarial service, so everything worked out for the best."

"What about her husband-to-be? The fellow in Hawaii."

"According to Janet, he's a convert to beach life, too."

"What's all this about a convert, Paige love?" came a booming voice behind them. "Who's the lucky man this time?"

Paige's head swiveled. "Thor! It's good to see you! I didn't know you started work this early."

"I'd have been here at the crack of dawn if I'd known you were back. Why didn't you call me?"

Paige grinned up at him. "One thing at a time, friend." Then, noticing that the man across the table had gotten to his feet, "Thor Goransen, Alan Bayne. Thor manages the Conquistador for his family," she went on in explanation as the men shook hands. "Mr. Bayne is staying in the annex for the next week or so."

"Janet didn't mention that," Thor said, looking surprised. "Mind if I join you?" he asked them, even as he motioned the waitress to bring another cup of coffee.

Paige watched as the two men settled in their chairs, unconsciously noting the differences between them. Next to Alan Bayne, Thor looked more like one of his Viking ancestors than usual. Where the visitor's hair was dark and under control, Thor's flaxen mop closely resembled a sheepdog cut. Thor's sport coat showed off his broad shoulders and the muscular development of his arms, while Alan's strength was kept under wraps and only the easy, fluid way he moved showed it. Both men topped six feet, but Thor's rawboned physique made him look considerably more formidable. For as long as Paige could remember, he had thoroughly enjoyed the admiring glances cast by his female guests, and she'd often teased him about the way he handled the more predatory women.

She could understand how he'd succeeded. Given the need, he could summon a shy, vulnerable image that defrosted the most militant female. Success had convinced him not to alter the role perceptibly. But as time passed, he abandoned wearing baggy-kneed jeans and T-shirts for romantic walks on the beach, appearing instead in tailored denims topped with a turtleneck sweater and expensive down vest.

Not having seen Thor for several months made Paige more observant than usual, and she decided that he was finally beginning to show every one of his thirty years—despite his beige silk sport coat and a smile that exuded hospitality.

His manner apparently wasn't having the desired effect on Alan, either, whose expression suggested that he'd swallowed some hemlock rather than the Conquistador's excellent coffee.

"I don't quite understand this," Thor said, a frown marring his broad forehead as he shifted to face Paige. "The grapevine had it that Seth went with your sister. I didn't think you'd be coming to the Cove."

"Somebody has to tote the barge and lift the bales, or is it the other way around?" she asked lightly. "I'm handling the business for Janet while she's gone."

His frown deepened. "Does 'Miss Practically Perfect' approve?"

It was an unkind reference to Liza, with whom he'd sparred for years, and Paige shook her head reprovingly. "Of course she does. As a matter of fact, we'll be dividing assignments. Mr. Bayne has some secretarial work he wants done."

Thor's big frame shook as he gave a shout of laughter. "Talk about the luck of the draw!" he told Alan. "You really came out ahead. At least you did in one way." He turned back to Paige. "I thought you couldn't take shorthand."

"It's been a while," Paige said, wishing he'd shut up, "but I expect it will come back to me."

"If it doesn't, just put on a pair of blinders," Thor advised Alan, "and call the other member of the firm. Liza can do anything—and she's the first to admit it."

"You're not being fair," Paige cut in, wondering how to change the subject. Of all the topics she hadn't wanted discussed, Liza's work habits headed the list. The way things were going, Alan Bayne would be stiff-necked about any division of future duties. And there was no telling how she'd broach the news of doing sex research to Liza. The other woman barely tolerated the existence of a masculine gender—and feeling the way she did, she'd be more apt to burn the manuscript than type it!

"What's so fascinating about that patch of ocean? It hasn't changed that I can see."

Thor's puzzled query made Paige look up hastily, only to discover both men surveying her, Thor with visible annoyance and Alan Bayne with what appeared to be resigned acceptance.

"I'm sorry," she stammered, aware that she was acting like a zombie again. "It was late when I got back from Portland last night—maybe I didn't have enough sleep."

"Have some more coffee," Alan suggested.

"Oh, no. I'm practically awash now. I drank some at the office before this," she added to Thor. "And I really should get back—Janet left a list of things to do."

Alan shoved back his own cup. "I'd like to get settled in the—what do you call it?"

"The annex," Paige supplied.

"So called because you're within whistling distance of your landlady," Thor told him. "That makes it convenient to handle complaints like leaking faucets and extra towels."

"If the landlady is at home," Paige added levelly. "But if you need much room service, you'd do better here at the Conquistador."

"I'll take my chances. Are you ready to go?" Alan asked her.

"Yes, thanks. Thor—it was nice to see you again."

"I know you too well for a polite brush-off like that. Your place or mine tonight?" he asked, a wicked gleam in his eye.

Paige was aware of Alan Bayne's sudden stillness beside her, and she could have cheerfully hit Thor over the head for deliberately embarrassing her. "If you're angling for a dinner invitation," she told him, stressing the last two words, "you're going about it in the wrong way."

"Even if I bring the steaks and a bottle of wine?"

She smiled reluctantly. "All right—but only because I'm tired of ninety-seven different ways to fix chicken."

His grin was unrepentant. "I counted on that. Six o'clock?"

"That should be fine. I'm hoping for a phone call from Janet about that time with a report on the wedding."

"Good! We'll toast her together."

Alan dropped some currency on the table for a tip and reached for the check. "It was nice meeting you, Mr. Goransen."

"Make it Thor," the other said, neatly forestalling him by capturing the bill. "My treat. Any friend of Paige's is welcome here."

Alan started to set the record straight on that score but Paige got in first, saying hastily, "I'll see you tonight then, Thor. Thanks for the coffee."

He bent to give her a quick and possessive kiss, winking before he disappeared through the swinging doors of the restaurant's kitchen.

"Quite a personality," Alan said, his voice carefully expressionless as they waited for the elevator to take them back to ground level.

Paige started to brush his comment aside and then changed her mind. It might not hurt to let him think that Thor was more than an old acquaintance. He'd find out soon enough that the man distributed kisses with casual abandon on practically any acceptable female within reach. She had no doubts that Thor mentioned the dinner invitation just to make sure that Alan didn't get any ideas along that line.

Not that he would, she decided, noting the steely set of his jaw as they went out to his parked car.

The trip back to the office was made with determined but sporadic attempts at conversation. They covered the possibility of rain before evening at some length and discussed the latest winter storms in the east before he finally drew up beside her car. She got out hastily and tried not to show her relief as she said, "If you'll follow me—the house is hardly any distance."

A terse jerk of his head was Alan's only response to that, and she sighed as she got in and started her car. Maybe it was a good thing for Janet's finances that he *had* paid in advance. The expression on his face ever since leaving the Conquistador showed that he wasn't impressed by the scenery, the weather, or the inhabitants of Cameron Cove.

She was glad to see a softening of his countenance when he pulled into the double carport at the house a little later.

"Your place?" he asked, getting out of the car and surveying the structure and grounds.

"Janet and I share ownership," she said, and gestured him toward a path which skirted the corner of it. "The annex is down this way. Do you want to bring your things?"

"I'll get them later," he said, following her on the partially covered walkway made of rough cedar. He gestured overhead. "A nice touch."

"And practical," she assured him. "Our weather is decidedly fickle next to the ocean. We share this garden area, but there's a balcony of your own if you

36

prefer privacy. Here we are." She paused in front of the low, rambling cottage of weathered cedar which matched the outer appearance of the larger house. "And an extra key," she said, handing it over after first opening the door with it. "I hope everything's all right."

He whistled softly in admiration as he followed her in the slate entryway and looked around. There was a magnificent view of the distant surf from the window wall with the balcony she'd mentioned. The compact but comfortable living room with its fireplace and black leather couch had a movable table for dining in the ell next to a red and chrome kitchen. Wooden window blinds picked up the color accents of the larger room, and the slate tiles led to the bedroom and bath down the hall.

"Very nice," Alan said after completing his inspection. "Very nice indeed. Much better than I hoped for."

Paige's pride was somewhat vindicated, but she was still smarting from his cool behavior on the ride from the Conquistador. "We've always liked it."

Her hauteur evidently amused him. "I don't suppose you'd want to sell it."

"I'm still trying to find a way to make a living here so I can be the permanent tenant," she told him, thawing slightly.

He leaned against the back of the big couch that faced the fireplace. "Who knows? This may be the start of a new career for you."

"You mean as a secretary?" When he merely

grinned, she probed further. "Is that what you had in mind?"

"I was thinking more of the research angle."

She straightened by the doorway. "I wanted to talk to you about that. You've come to the wrong place if you think I'm hoping for some sort of cheap thrill."

"It never occurred to me." He shook his head reprovingly. "The working of the female mind never ceases to amaze me. You surely don't think that there's anything wrong with sex?"

"Of course not, but . . ."

"Or writing about it?" he cut in.

"Well, no, but . . ."

"Or talking about it. . . ?"

"Will you stop!" she flared, her voice rising. "You don't need to make me sound like a repressed virgin. You know very well what I mean. And if you don't stop grilling me, I'll-I'll—"

"You'll what?"

Paige scowled fiercely at his relaxed form, wishing with all her soul that she could tell him to find himself another secretary in the next county. But she couldn't and he knew it. Knew it very well because Janet had confessed just the night before that her part of Alan Bayne's check had paid for her airline ticket to the islands and most of her trousseau.

"Well?" he asked when the silence lengthened.

She let out her breath and wilted visibly.

"I think you're allowing your imagination to run away with you," he said in such a reasonable tone that she wanted to pick up the ceramic ashtray from the end table and heave it at him. "I'm not planning to write any 'how to' sex tome," he went on. "But from what I see on the newsstands these days, purple passion is either what the readers want or what they're being given. There's no point in trying to buck the tide."

"Exactly what kind of books do you write?" Paige asked, her tone still frigid.

"Adventure stories, mainly. I don't earn my living in front of a typewriter, but it's paid off as a sideline. With an enlarged format, it might do even better. That's where you come in."

"You mean doing research?"

He nodded. "I want you to skim the current competition for me. See how much sex figures in the plot and what kind is the most popular."

"What kind?" she asked faintly.

"That's right." He sounded impatient. "Anatomy, physical details—that sort of stuff. Frankly, I think it detracts from the plot line, but if that's what publishers want, that's what I'll give them. You can devote your mornings to research and the afternoons to typing the manuscript."

"But that's working full-time!"

"Certainly." He folded his arms across his chest as he surveyed her. "I thought I made that clear in my letter to your sister."

"Which means that I'll *have* to call in Liza," Paige said, thinking aloud as she tried to remember what else Janet had left on the agenda.

"That's up to you. Now, if you don't mind—I'll see about getting unpacked." He got unhurriedly to his feet and came over to open the front door beside her. "Incidentally, I'd like to get started right away."

"You mean today?"

He looked at her as if amazed that any person could be so thick-headed, and his response was slow and distinct—so she couldn't possibly misunderstand. "That's right. Today. After lunch. Shall we say one o'clock?"

She swallowed and nodded, allowing herself to be ushered out onto the front porch as she tried to assimilate it. Then another thought occurred. "But where?"

"What do you mean—where?"

"Where do I work?"

He grinned suddenly. "I think the current expression is—your place or mine?"

Which was his way of reminding her he hadn't forgotten Thor's gibe, she thought mutinously.

Alan's grin disappeared at her frozen response. He sounded terse as he said, "That's up to you. Now that I think of it, we'd better reverse the schedule today. You can spend this afternoon on the researching bit." His hand was on his wallet as he spoke and he held out a crisp twenty-dollar bill.

"What's that for?" she asked suspiciously, unwilling to take it.

"The kind of books I was talking about," he said, sounding as if his patience were running thin. "I doubt if you have many of them in stock."

"You mean the kind with the 'rapture in the pasture' covers?" She took the bill he was holding and put it in her coat pocket. "You're right. The books in the house belong to Janet and Seth. She only reads biographies and he's on a sci-fi tangent right now." She lingered an instant longer to ask, "What kind of notes do you want me to take?"

"I'll leave that to you. Underline the best descriptive paragraphs and be prepared to report on exactly what . . ." He hesitated, obviously searching for a diplomatic phrase.

". . . what turns me on?" she finished for him drily. "You don't have to draw pictures. I am twenty-four years old and I know that babies don't appear under cabbage leaves."

"That will make it easier. I'll see you tomorrow morning, then. If you don't like an electric portable—better bring another typewriter along." With that admonition, he closed the front door firmly behind her, leaving her still standing on the step.

Chapter Three

Liza Strom looked up from the electric typewriter at Janet's desk when Paige let herself into the office later that afternoon.

"I thought you said you weren't coming in again today," she accused, turning off the machine and letting her hands fall in her lap. "Did I get my signals mixed?"

Paige shook her head as she dumped the armful of books she was carrying on the edge of the desk. "No—you're in the right place. I'm not so sure about me. Either I'm on overload or senility is setting in early."

"I just made some fresh coffee, if that would make you feel better." The other woman waved her hand toward the percolator.

"It couldn't hurt." Paige unzipped the down jacket she was wearing over her jeans and walked over to help herself. "Don't let me interrupt if that typing's due out."

Liza shrugged, reaching for her pile of completed copy and original catalogue sheets with penciled corrections. "I can read proof and talk to you at the same time."

"In that case, I'll warm your coffee,'" Paige said, grinning at the other's matter-of-fact tone. Considering Liza's brusque manner, it was as close to an invitation as she'd ever get. Most times, she rarely stopped typing long enough to acknowledge a greeting.

Paige surveyed Janet's assistant surreptitiously as she took care of the coffee and extracted a tin of butter cookies from the bottom drawer of a file cabinet. Liza shook her head decisively at the cookie offer and took a sip of black coffee instead. Such will power accounted for her trim figure, Paige knew, although Liza kept her measurements well concealed with her usual outfit of a too-large black sweater worn with burgundy slacks. Her brown hair was pulled severely back in a braid and secured by a rubber band. Only her flawless skin and heavily fringed blue eyes made people take a second look. But even those assets couldn't disguise the fact that she'd recently turned the shady side of thirty and was doing her darnedest to look forty.

At that moment, Liza's expression was even more stern than usual as she noticed Paige's books. "Your tastes in reading have certainly changed since the last time I saw you," she said disparagingly.

"That's what Mr. Johnson down at the drug store

said when I bought them," Paige agreed. "Just think what he'd have thought if I told him they were required reading."

Her casual comment bought Liza's head up from the proofs abruptly. "Required for what? A new course at the Experimental College?"

Paige started to laugh. "You mean they have those classes here, too?"

"Some summer visitors tried to schedule that kind of a sandbox series, but they couldn't make it pay so they gave up and went back to San Francisco."

"That sounds like Cameron Cove. I'll have to tell my new employer that the best-seller here features agate and clam beds rather than four-posters. Of course, there might be a way to jazz up the tide tables."

"You mean that Alan Bayne wanted you to buy those books?" Liza looked as nonplussed as her efficient nature would allow. "I must say, he didn't seem the type."

"I don't know what kind of a type you're talking about. Besides, I thought you didn't know the man."

"I don't. Not really. I just happened to see him unloading his car when I was coming back here after lunch. You know how I always take a half-hour walk? Well, today I decided to walk past your house. Naturally, when I saw him in the carport, I stopped and introduced myself. Especially since he'd asked us to have a typewriter delivered tomorrow."

Paige frowned as she cradled the warm coffee mug between her palms. "He certainly doesn't leave anything to chance. Did he mention the kind of a book he's writing?"

"We didn't get down to specifics. He was just polite and said all the right things about the local scenery. Are you sure he's going to write one of those?" She pointed a neatly filed but unvarnished fingernail at the pile of books.

"That's the general idea."

"Umm. He's probably just doing it for the money."

Paige decided there wasn't any use trying to convince Liza that Alan Bayne wasn't all true-blue. She got up and rinsed out her coffee mug in the tiny stainless steel sink.

"Did Thor reach you?" Liza's voice was offhand as she bent over her lists again.

"About an hour ago. He's coming to dinner and wanted to say that he'd be a little late. Since he's bringing the main course, I thought it was nice of him."

Liza's sniff showed what she thought of that. "I'm surprised he could fit you into his schedule so soon. He's been playing a redhead from Portland off against a blonde artist who's just moved here from California."

"Which means I'll probably hear all about both of them before we've finished the main course tonight. One of these days he'll have to settle down—his social life must cost him a fortune."

Liza nodded grimly and gestured again toward the novels that Paige was retrieving. "I don't know why you bothered with those—just ask Thor for a few tips. From what I hear, he could write a series of books."

"And I'll bet that he's the one who spread most of the rumors," Paige said, amused. "You know better than to believe that malarkey."

"There's no need to whitewash his reputation for my benefit. Besides, you haven't been around here lately."

Paige's smile widened. "Well, if he makes a pass I can put it to good use." At Liza's uncomprehending scowl, she went on to explain. "I'll take notes. That should stop him cold. Not only that, it will impress your friend Mr. Bayne."

"How's that?" Liza was wide-eyed, by then.

"I'll put it down on my time sheet as field research with double rates for overtime."

Liza emitted an unladylike snort. "If it works, you're in the wrong business. Don't expect me to hold your hand if nobody cooperates."

"I'd be more apt to need help if they did," Paige shifted her load of books in her arms to open the door. "I'll check with you in the morning."

"Send Janet my best if you talk to her."

"I'll do that, and give you a full report on the wedding if she floats down from the clouds long enough to phone."

As it happened, Janet's long distance call came through almost simultaneously with the ringing of the doorbell that evening. Paige picked up the receiver and said urgently, "Could you hold on, please," before making a dash for the front door. She gestured Thor in and told him, "I'm on the phone—

make yourself at home," then hurried back to pick up the receiver in the bedroom.

Ten minutes later, she found him in the kitchen inspecting the contents of the refrigerator while two plastic-wrapped porterhouse steaks reposed on the counter. "I'm sorry about the interruption," she said, reaching for an apron to protect her brown velveteen skirt and polished cotton blouse. "That was Janet and I had to hear all the wedding news. They were just married this afternoon, and she was still so excited that I could hardly sort out the details. John wasn't much better, but Seth made up for the two of them."

Thor closed the refrigerator and leaned against it. "You mean there are going to be three for the honeymoon! Thought Janet had more sense."

Paige frowned, suddenly aware that he needed the refrigerator as a necessary prop. "Seth's going to stay with John's sister for a few days. Apparently Janet isn't the only one who's been celebrating."

A foolish grin came over his handsome features, and he ran his fingers through his hair, trying to smooth it. "Sorry, sweetie. I met a man this afternoon and the hospitality got a little out of hand."

"So I gather." Her glance went to his white blazer, which was buttoned askew. It wasn't a glaring fault because his gray sport shirt and slacks were immaculate. Evidently he'd changed for his dinner date before the cocktail hour.

"Some food'll do the trick." He rubbed his forehead wearily. "Who'd have thought the ol' geezer'd have a hollow leg?"

"Why don't you sit down over here and keep me company," she suggested, taking his arm and steering him to a chair by the table. "There's leftover potato soup for starters. . . ."

He grimaced but sat down. "No black coffee routine?"

"Nope. I'll have some soup with you while I'm making the salad," she said. "I certainly don't need any more coffee today."

"Who needs food? This is better," he said, pulling her onto his lap before she could turn away.

"Thor, stop it! Let go of me."

"Now, sweetie, jus' hold still so I can kiss you," he ordered, wrapping his arms even tighter around her waist.

His kiss landed at the corner of her mouth as she managed to turn her head, but when she would have pulled away, she found that the starched lace belt on her apron had tangled with a button on his sport coat.

Thor started to laugh as he discovered her quandary. "That'll teach you! Now it'll cost you a couple of kisses before I let you loose."

"Idiot!" Paige said resignedly, not able to stay angry under his smug glance. "The things I do for a steak dinner—" her voice broke off as three distinct knocks sounded on the back door nearby. She drew in her breath sharply as she beheld Alan's stern countenance through the glass at the top. "Thor, for heaven's sake—let me up," she said, trying to get to her feet. "What's he going to think?"

"Who cares?" Thor squinted, trying to unwrap

the thread from his coat button. "Damn if I can see—I'll jus' rip it off."

"No!" Her voice rose. "Here—I'll take off the apron and we can sort it out later." She managed to undo the bow at her back and slid out of the apron, leaving it on his lap as she hurried to open the back door. "I'm sorry," she told Alan breathlessly. "We had a small problem."

"So I gathered." Alan nodded distantly to Thor who made a halfhearted attempt to get to his feet and then subsided in the chair again. "I'm sorry to interrupt."

"You didn't," Paige informed him. "I mean—there wasn't anything going on. My apron got caught on Thor's coat button."

"My dear girl, you don't have to explain anything to me," Alan said, clearly annoyed to be involved in any confessionals.

For some reason, his remark appealed to Thor's sense of humor and he let out a guffaw. "Take it from me," he said, giving Alan an owllike leer, "tha's not the way to talk to a woman. 'N I should know. They call me the local Loth–Loth . . ."

"I get the idea," Alan cut in, and turned back to Paige. "Would you mind if I had another key made for the annex? A friend of mine has just arrived in town."

". . . and it's his fault that I'm out of shape," Thor interrupted, his head still bent over the offending button.

Alan's head swiveled back to the other man. "What did you say?"

Thor straightened his shoulders and spoke with unnecessary care, "I said that it's your buddy's fault I had more than my quota at the bar. You don' need to worry, though. He got back to his room okay. Great guy, ol' George."

Alan's dark eyebrows were a solid line of displeasure. "Exactly where did you meet 'old George'?"

"This afternoon at the bar. He got lonely up in his room after you left him but he's okay now. I took care of him."

"If it's not too much trouble," Paige said to Alan, "would you mind telling me who this 'old George' is that we're talking about?"

"Apparently you weren't in the Conquistador bar this afternoon," he said wryly.

"No, but maybe I should have been. After leafing through my required reading, I could have used a stiff drink." She went over to the refrigerator, pulling out an ovenware container of leftover soup, which she put on the stove. "Was that George's trouble, too?"

Thor spoke up before Alan could reply. "I *told* you—he was lonesome. Now he knows lotsa people—friends of mine."

"That's just great," Alan said without enthusiasm, before asking Paige, "Is it all right if he uses my duplicate key for the time being?"

"He'll have to until you get another one made at the hardware store. Will this George . . ."

At her hesitation, Alan filled in the gaps. "George Porter. He's a business acquaintance who's been working too hard. I thought he'd enjoy some ocean fishing for a break. It would be convenient if he could drop in here and not have to go back to the Conquistador for every little thing."

"Don' have to worry about that," Thor said, determined not to be overlooked. "I tol' George 'bout my cruiser at Depoe Bay. He can use it anytime."

"That isn't necessary. I wouldn't want you to go to any trouble . . ."

Alan was cut off in mid-sentence. "No trouble," Thor said, reveling in his role. "I charter the boat off 'n on. Jus' leave it to me."

"You might as well give up," Paige said, feeling a certain sympathy for Alan under the circumstances. "Thor can overrule every objection. Besides, your friend George will have a good time. It's a very nice cruiser."

Thor nodded, bundling up the apron, which he'd finally managed to detach from his coat, and putting it on the table beside him. "When's soup goin' to be ready?"

"Any minute," Paige said, checking it on the stove. She looked hesitantly toward the other man. "There's enough for an extra bowl."

"No, thanks." Alan was so definite that he was scarcely polite. When he saw the color rise in her cheeks, he added in a more agreeable tone, "I've made other plans."

"I hope they don' involve George. The last I heard, he was flat out on the bed in his room," Thor announced.

"I'll remember that." Alan turned to Paige. "About that extra key—I'll have another one made and turn it in when I leave." As he started toward the door again, he gestured toward her pile of books on the end of the counter. "Your homework?"

"That's right."

He paused with his hand on the doorknob. "You don't sound enthralled with your work."

"What kind of work's he talking about?" Thor asked in a querulous voice as he got to his feet.

"I'll explain later. Sit down and I'll serve your soup," Paige said hastily.

Alan opened the door, saying to her in a low tone, "I'll see you in the morning. But if you have any trouble, I'll be around for a while."

"What kind of trouble?" Paige asked, annoyed.

Alan stepped out onto the back step, jerking his head toward the part of the kitchen where Thor was sprawled in his chair. "The two-footed kind. You looked as if you needed a helping hand when I first arrived. Or maybe you don't mind being mauled by a drunk."

Paige drew herself up indignantly. "That's a hateful thing to say. Thor's a friend of mine, and he doesn't make a habit of drinking."

"He's all yours, then." Alan craned his head to check out the kitchen before adding brusquely, "You'd better get back in there because your soup's starting to boil over."

A few minutes later, after Paige had pulled the soup off the burner and cleaned the top of the stove, she discovered that Alan had gone—thankfully without any more advice.

Thor, once he'd consumed the soup and worked

his way through steak and salad, reverted to his normal manner. But aside from mentioning that her Alan Bayne didn't go out of his way to win friends, he seemed content to ignore the other's visit.

Paige felt the same way except for one matter that needed to be set straight. "He's not 'my' Alan Bayne," she told him decidedly. "He's simply here on business for a while. You must have gathered that we don't exactly hit it off."

"It did cross my mind," Thor said, watching her clear the table before pouring their coffee. "Don't let it spoil your homecoming, though. According to old George, Bayne doesn't expect to be here any longer than absolutely necessary. They're strictly big-city types."

His announcement didn't do anything to improve Paige's disposition. She poured their coffee carefully, but when he would have taken it in the living room to drink in front of the fireplace, she said, "I should warn you. This will have to be an early night."

"You're not mad at me, are you, love? Just because I was a little bent out of shape when I came."

"It's not that—although don't make it a habit," she told him with a level look.

"Now you sound like Prim and Prissy."

Paige sighed irritably. "Is that a relative of old George?"

"I'm talking about Liza." Thor looked at her with concern. "You must be tired."

"I am. Besides, you shouldn't talk like that. Liza's a very nice woman..."

". . . who's disliked me for years. Fortunately, the feeling's mutual."

Paige shook her head. "You two have been feuding longer than the Montagues and the Capulets. Why don't you bury the hatchet, for heaven's sake?"

"No way. I wouldn't go within ten feet of that woman if she had a hatchet in her hand. It's bad enough the rest of the time." Thor waggled his empty coffee cup. "Do I get a refill before you kick me out?"

"Help yourself." Paige watched him wander over to the percolator, detouring to examine her stack of newly purchased paperbacks.

His thick eyebrows went up as he inspected a thinly clad heroine on the top cover. "That's some kind of homework. What does Bayne want, for God's sake?"

"It's research for a novel he's writing," Paige said briefly, hoping he'd let the matter drop with that.

Naturally Thor didn't cooperate. He took a sip of coffee before bringing his cup back to the table, saying meanwhile, "George told me your chum wrote adventure stores. Who's kidding who?"

"I haven't the foggiest idea, and he hasn't shown me any manuscript. All I know is that his fee paid for Janet's airplane ticket—among other things. Does that answer your question?"

"Temper, temper. You're beginning to sound like Liza." Thor rumpled her hair before sitting down again. "Old George said Bayne hit the jackpot with his second novel. Over a million in paperback, but he still doesn't like to write full-time."

Paige whistled softly, impressed despite herself. "Now I remember! It was an espionage story a while back. Film rights and everything. My boss mentioned reading it."

"So why does somebody like that need to research heroines who enjoy debauchery?" Thor leaned forward, his eyes teasing. "You're sure it wasn't your idea?"

"Very sure," she said drily.

"Too bad. I was going to volunteer some practical instruction along that line to help you out."

"It's such a pleasure to meet a modest man; no wonder Liza wants to stick pins in you." She picked up his cup and saucer and took them to sink, brushing her palms together afterward as if that ended the matter.

"I get the picture." Thor picked up his sweater and tossed it over his shoulder. "Never mind, you may need a friendly man around the house sooner than you think. I'd say your current occupant in the annex is one cold customer."

Paige held open the door. "Just the way I like it. Thanks for the steaks."

"And thanks for sobering me up—I think." Thor gave her his specialty—a slow, crooked smile which was hard to resist. "See you tomorrow."

"Let's wait and see. 'Night, Thor." She stood on tiptoe to brush a friendly kiss over his cheek and stepped back quickly before he could make a last-minute stand, managing to close the door firmly in the process.

Either the evening's menu or the happenings

weren't conducive to sound sleep and she spent a restless night, awakening at what seemed to be every gust of wind brushing the shrubbery against the side of the house. When the first ribbons of dawn lighted the sky, she groaned slightly and wondered why she hadn't pulled the drapes completely shut. On the other hand, she reasoned, if she got up to close them she'd really be wide awake. Another possibility was to get up and have a relaxing walk on the beach before any other people had the same idea.

She stepped out onto the balcony for a moment to decide whether the clear weather would last and mentally registered the noise of a truck engine in the still morning air. The low, grinding sound brought another vision to mind and she muttered abruptly, "Seth's rocks! Damn! I forgot all about them!"

She snatched a yellow terry robe from the foot of the bed and stepped into a pair of matching scuffs. Pushing her hair back from her face with a careless hand, she hurried through the house and out to the adjoining carport. There, tucked away on a counter, a small rock tumbler was revolving with a monotonous whirring sound. She hastily unplugged it and managed to dislodge a metal can of paint thinner onto the cement floor in the process. Fortunately, the can was securely capped, and she pushed it out of the way in order to approach the tumbler more easily.

She was unscrewing the nut on top of the barrel when she heard steps along the path, and Alan stuck his head into the carport.

"What the deuce . . ." he began, and then shook

his head disbelievingly. "Do you usually go on cleaning sprees at the crack of dawn?"

"Always," she said, trying to hide her chagrin at being discovered in such a homely outfit. Not that Alan looked much better. He was unshaven and had obviously dragged on a pair of jeans over his pajamas without bothering to tuck in the top. His attire gave her the courage to ask, "Why? Did I interrupt something?"

"Just sleep." At her sudden look of dismay, he shook his head ruefully and said, "Sorry. I didn't mean that. I was already wandering around my balcony when I heard a disturbance out here."

"I managed to knock over this"—she indicated the gallon can with her slipper—"when I unplugged the tumbler. I'd make a terrible second-story man."

The shadow of a grin passed over his face. "Well, it would be hard for the neighbors to overlook you in that bright yellow robe." Then, before she could reply, he came closer to peer over her shoulder at the tumbler. "So that's the noise I heard going out here."

She nodded. "My nephew has a batch of agates inside and I promised to watch over them while he's away. The mix should have been changed yesterday, but I forgot until a few minutes ago."

"Is the deadline so critical that you have to do it right now?" He sounded genuinely puzzled.

"You mean, without bothering to get dressed first?" She laughed and shook her head. "Of course not. I just reacted impulsively when I remembered. A failing of mine," she added wryly, and tightened the belt on her robe. "The agates will still be here after breakfast."

"I see." He rested a hip against the counter. "Do you allow an audience for the unveiling?"

"Are you serious?"

"As a matter of fact, I am." His diffident smile made him look younger and, with his dark unshaven jawline, almost piratical.

Which showed how much she needed a sobering cup of coffee, Paige told herself. Soon she'd be thinking that he was halfway human!

Her hesitation evidently conveyed a different reaction in Alan. "It isn't at all important," he said, his smile fading when Paige forgot to say, "Of course you can watch," as she'd planned—even framing a breakfast invitation in the bargain.

"I'm sorry," she said hastily, "I don't function on all cylinders at this hour. I'd be glad if you'd look on, but I should warn you—it's contagious."

He frowned, his thick eyebrows drawing together again. "What is?"

"Well, the next symptom is going out to hunt for agates like the rest of us." She grinned mischievously. "You didn't think we stroll the beaches in the rain just for fresh air, did you?"

His features softened. "I'm learning fast. Do you suppose we can work some beach walks into our schedule?"

"You mean that's going to be part of the research?" Her voice rose in disbelief.

"There are other things possible on a beach besides agate hunting," he said solemnly. "Like the symbolism of nature and human emotions. Or the possibilities of character confrontation on an isolated strip of sand. That could make the dialogue more provocative."

"If you're thinking of having your characters making mad love behind a piece of driftwood, you'll have to choose another locale," she told him, unimpressed. "The members of our volunteer beach patrol would be stumbling over them, and they don't approve of *anything* that changes the environment."

He shrugged and put his hands in his pockets. "So the lead characters get together afterward. The time and place don't matter. Besides, the way I feel now, a cup of coffee is the only thing that could raise my pulse rate."

"While you're still at a safe low ebb, would you like to come to breakfast?"

Her impulsive invitation caught him halfway down the path. He turned to survey her levelly. "No passion over the poached eggs?"

"Just toast under them. And grapefruit. And coffee. In about—"

He looked at his watch. "Twenty minutes?"

"Make it twenty-five."

"Fair enough. Afterward we'll check out the agates."

Paige's pulse rate zoomed under his amused glance. "Do you mean these in the tumbler or the ones still on the beach?"

His grin flashed again. "I mean the ones behind the driftwood logs—damned if my hero is going to be stopped by any beach patrol."

It all seemed too good to be true, and that was the way it turned out. Barely ten minutes later, when Paige was turning off the water after her shower, the phone rang demandingly.

"Hullo," she responded on the fourth ring, out of breath because of her dash from the bathroom.

"Paige—I mean Miss Kendall. It's Alan Bayne. I'm sorry, but something's come up." He paused, obviously trying for a diplomatic way of letting her down.

Why didn't he just say that it was no go, she thought rebelliously. Probably he'd had second thoughts about putting their acquaintance on a more informal level and was scratching for a plausible excuse.

"It's George," he said finally, "and he's suffering from the grandfather of all hangovers this morning. You and I seem destined to sober up our friends."

Paige felt a little better. Absently wiping a drop of moisture from the telephone table with the end of her towel, she said, "I don't suppose that he'd want either breakfast or a walk on the beach."

"I'm afraid not. Maybe you'll give me a rain check."

"Of course. What about this afternoon? Do I still follow the same schedule?"

Impatience crept back into his voice. "You'd better get started with my rough draft. I'll leave the first chapters on the table. An original and one copy will do."

"What if I can't read your writing?"

"It's a typed draft so you'll only have to worry

about my editing corrections. I'll leave a sample page to show you the margins and physical layout."

"All right." She hoped that her voice didn't sound as dubious about the prospect as she felt. "Is there any place where I can reach you if I get stuck?"

"Not today." There was a perceptible pause before he added diffidently, "I'm sorry to miss that tumbler changeover."

For a minute Paige couldn't think what he meant. Then she said drily, "It's not as if we're working with the Kohinoor or the Star of India. I'll change the mix tomorrow or the next day. Seth's agates will just be more polished than usual."

"Great! I'd appreciate it!"

It was strange that he hadn't exhibited that enthusiasm when he was talking about his manuscript, Paige thought. From what she'd heard, most writers regarded their creations with a fierce protective pride—not pages left casually on the table with the hope that a strange typist could decipher them.

Alan's brusque, "Is there anything else?" brought her abruptly back to the present.

"Not that I can think of," she said, trying to sound like a proper employee when she didn't feel like anything of the kind.

"Then I'll see you tomorrow—if not before." The last three words were clearly an afterthought, but he might as well have said, "Don't count on it."

So much for all her high hopes, she thought as she put the receiver down. She stared blankly at it as she wiped off wet fingermarks with her towel and sighed over the path her wet footprints had left on the rug. Suddenly, everything had taken a turn for the worse.

"Damnation," she muttered violently, and stomped off to get dressed.

When she emerged in jeans and a plaid shirt a few minutes later, she had decided that bacon and eggs were too much trouble to cook for one person. She settled for toast and coffee, which she ate looking out over the rocky beach of the inner cove.

She debated thoughts of a walk along the beach and then realized that she was merely trying to postpone her required reading. Carefully checking the time, she brought the pile of books into the living room and delved into the top one. There weren't any interruptions after that, and Paige resolutely skimmed through the volumes, taking notes when she'd hit an interesting paragraph or a unique plot angle that the author had used to fit in a steamy passage.

Finally, after three hours of solid reading, she closed the book she'd been reading and tossed it to the other end of the couch. That particular story really deserved to be tossed into the wastebasket, she decided, and went in to reheat the coffee—anything to get the dregs of that last story line out of her mind. For a hundred and fifty pages she'd been reading about a so-called hero who leaped from bed to bed, matched with a heroine who also spent most of her time between the sheets. The writer held the sexual extravaganza together with a plot thinner than the heroine's nightgown, and the "story" was tossed aside with just as much abandon. The sexual exploits required a physical dexterity beyond belief, and occupied so much of the characters' days and nights that it was a wonder they didn't collapse in the third chapter from starvation, if not exhaustion. Unfortunately, their exploits didn't hold the same fascination for Paige, who had gotten up at one point to open a bag of potato chips and another time to watch the garbage truck making its weekly rounds.

Later, when drinking her solitary cup of coffee, she concluded that purple passion didn't do much for a reader in the cold morning light. She was tired of descriptive paragraphs about heroes' hairy chests and even more tired of the heroines' voluptuous alabaster ones.

In the historicals, action occasionally recessed to the dining room, where novelists faithfully chronicled every item their characters consumed during eight-course meals. The latest repast telling of roast goose followed by prawns and a giblet pie forced Paige to put away her bag of potato chips. She was still shuddering over thoughts of that giblet pie when the phone rang, and she went thankfully to answer it.

"Paige, love!" Thor said, sounding his usual brisk self. "I called to invite you to lunch."

"Oh, no . . ." She swallowed and added apologetically, "I feel as if I'd been eating all morning. Thanks all the same."

"Well, if you're not hungry, how about a game of tennis? The rain should hold off for an hour or two."

Paige cast a glance toward the window, realizing that she hadn't given the weather a thought for most of the morning. As Thor said, the clouds were threatening but the sun was still managing to hold its own.

"Well, what do you say?"

"I'm sorry, Thor." Paige couldn't blame him for sounding impatient. "It's tempting but I'd better not weaken. After all, I'm supposed to be working, and I can imagine what my boss would think if he drove past the tennis courts and saw me."

"Not much chance of that. I know for a fact that he drove off in the other direction just a little while ago. Besides, he had very attractive company."

"I thought he was going out with old George." The words were out before Paige realized and she hurried to add, "Not that it makes any difference, of course."

"Of course." Thor didn't bother to hide his sarcasm. "Well, he had George along, but he seemed a lot more interested in the brunette next to him in the front seat. She looked vaguely familiar."

"Don't tell me there's one around here who's not in your little book."

"Now and then it happens. Sure you won't change your mind?"

"About the tennis? I'd better not. If you're serious about wanting a game, Liza might be tempted. She's really good."

"No, thanks. After she mopped the court with me, I'd be lectured about not putting in a full day of work. Just as if that would make any difference to my banker."

Paige realized that the discussion had taken a

wrong turn. Hastily she said, "Give me a rain check, will you? I'll ask about taking some time off when I see Mr. Bayne again—so I won't need to feel guilty about it."

"Damned if I can tell why you have to be such an eager beaver. It isn't as if it's your real job." Then, before she could defend herself, he said, "Forget it. Maybe it's just as well. My head feels as if it could fall off any minute, and fresh air might be the lethal blow."

"You mean it's the morning after the night before?"

"Why bring that up? I'll call you tomorrow, so save some time for me."

When he'd hung up, Paige replaced her own receiver and wandered in the kitchen to make a peanut butter sandwich. Even the pale sunlight was too good to waste, she decided impulsively, and opted for an impromptu beach picnic. She wrapped the sandwich in plastic and tucked it in the pocket of her down jacket before setting off toward the shore. She only walked to the edge of the cove but found a convenient driftwood log to sit on where she could enjoy a view of the surf while she ate.

Even that short lunch break made her approach her afternoon tasks with renewed vigor. She found the manuscript on the table where Alan had promised to leave it, along with an almost new typewriter and a supply of paper.

Her first glance at the rough draft showed her that she needn't have worried. The typing was straightforward, and only the scribbled corrections in the margin made her slow her copying speed. It was nice to discover that Alan had a splendid, terse style of writing that captured the reader's attention from the very first. His characters were realistic and extremely likable. But the most refreshing aspect so far as she was concerned was that, in the first chapter at least, the hero's bedroom was used strictly for sleeping.

The time passed quickly and she gathered her completed copy together for a final check in her own living room. It was approaching the dinner hour and she didn't want Alan to find her lingering in his living room if he should return. Not that she really expected him to entertain his brunette to a home-cooked dinner. He wasn't the type, she told herself, as she peered into her own refrigerator a little later.

Suddenly the prospect of an egg on toast or a frozen dinner sounded appalling, and she decided to go into Cameron Cove and give one of the fast-food outlets her business.

She patronized the nearest drive-in and settled behind a newspaper in the car while she ate her hamburger. Normally she would have chosen a paperback book for company, but her morning's required reading prompted her to choose the local news for relaxation instead.

Darkness was enveloping the horizon when she pulled back into her driveway and carport. It didn't surprise her to see that Alan's parking place was still vacant, but it didn't help her morale either. She couldn't expect that he would be having as quick an evening meal as she'd managed. More likely he'd be enjoying the scenic view from some local restaurant dining room and, if Thor's information were reliable, in very pleasant company.

She tried to push that knowledge to the back of her mind as she lit a fireplace fire for comfort and, once she'd pulled the screen against sparks, settled back on the davenport to read proof on the copy which she'd typed during the afternoon.

It was remarkably free of typos, and she smiled with satisfaction once she'd made the necessary corrections.

She weighed the completed copy in her hand, debating whether to take it across to the annex and have it ready for Alan when he returned or wait and deliver it first thing in the morning. The possibility that he'd want to check it as soon as he got in the house influenced her decision, and she briskly got out her passkey. This way, he wouldn't have any cause for complaint, and it would also quash the chance that he'd come calling to pick up his story. One view of her scruffy-looking yellow robe was quite enough for the day!

She walked swiftly down the winding path, glad that a few strategically placed spotlights at ground level provided soft illumination for the inner patio. The only light on the front porch of the annex came from a doorbell buzzer next to the knob, and she fumbled for an instant or two before inserting her key in the lock.

The heavy door creaked slightly as it opened. Paige decided that she'd have to put some oil on the decorative hinges even as she stepped into the foyer and fumbled for the hall switch.

It must have been instinct that told her she wasn't alone as her fingers finally reached and flipped on the light. As the bulb illuminated the foyer, she drew in her breath and abruptly turned toward the still-dark living room where she'd typed all afternoon.

A split second later, she felt movement from the closet door behind her. Before she could turn to check on it, a cloth was shoved over her face. At the same time a heavy hand came down painfully on her shoulder.

Her scream of terror turned into a muffled gurgle as strong fingers kept the cloth tight, and before she could get her hands up to struggle, she was shoved head first into the closet. The door slammed behind her, with the key clicking in the lock an instant later.

Paige took a shuddering breath at being free again. Then, abruptly, reality returned and she whirled in the darkness to pound on the locked door. "Let me out of here! Do you hear me? Let me out!"

In response, there was only the muffled sound of footsteps on the slate foyer, the creak of the hinges, and then a reverberating thud as the outer door was closed with finality.

After that, nothing.

Chapter Four

When she realized that there was no hope for an immediate rescue, Paige's knees buckled and she slithered in a heap to the closet floor. Her head seemed to be enveloped in plastic garment bags, which puzzled her until she remembered that the space was often used for overflow storage. Then another more vital problem occurred and she cautiously ran her fingers along the bottom of the door. When she discovered at least a half-inch of clearance, she uttered a sigh of relief.

She could no more have figured the amount of available oxygen in the crowded closet than she could have plotted a NASA expedition to Mars, but the knowledge that air was seeping in from the hallway helped quiet her mind.

That only left the possibility that whoever had shoved her in the closet in the first place might return. She grimaced in the darkness as she considered it. Then she squirmed around to prop herself against the door, trying to find a position that was halfway tolerable, even as her mind considered more unpleasant eventualities. Which was silly, she told herself finally. If whoever-it-was had wanted to silence her, he'd plenty of opportunity, since she'd evidently interrupted the vandal or petty thief in the midst of looting the house. She groaned and rested her head against her knees while thinking about it. If Alan's belongings had been rifled, she couldn't blame him if he moved out posthaste. Not only that, from now on she'd be looking over her shoulder herself. And that had never been a problem at Cameron Cove. It had only been lately that town doors had been locked as well as closed, Janet had reported.

Paige managed to massage her shoulder and tried to ignore the certain knowledge that the closet air was getting stuffier all the time. There was no reason to panic, she told herself firmly. Alan Bayne would be home soon, and all she had to do was beat on the door when she heard his key in the lock.

She was able to keep a rough idea of the time by the chiming of the mantel clock, and when an hour had passed, she decided to pull down a padded jacket from a hanger to make a rough bed on the floor. There was no point in suffering unduly, and the fact that the air seemed fresher at the bottom of the door was reason enough.

Surely she couldn't be stuck there much longer, she rationalized when the clock had chimed still another half-hour. By then, reaction had set in with a vengeance, and her imagination had the thief coming back to eliminate any eyewitnesses.

She was so deep in that fantasy that when the front door hinges creaked, it took a moment for her to realize that someone had actually come back into the house. The question was—who?

She stayed frozen in a ball on the floor when a sliver of light showed and the closet doorknob turned. There was a muttered epithet before a key rasped in the lock and she looked up, blinking, at the male figure towering over her.

"Don't step on me!" she protested, coming to life as his shoe collided with her thigh.

"What the hell!" Her warning caught Alan off balance, and he moved back so fast that he had to hang onto the doorjamb for support. "My Lord, what are you doing down there?"

The last came as she struggled to get up and discovered that one foot had gone to sleep, forcing her to subside on the floor again. And then, relieved to find that it really was Alan standing there, she indulged in the luxury of losing her temper. "That's the silliest question I've ever heard," she said crossly. "What do you think I'm doing?"

"Damned if I know." He frowned as he saw her grimace and massage her ankle. "What's the matter? Why didn't you say you were hurt?"

"Because I'm not. My foot's asleep, that's all. I've been here so long."

"Hang on—I'll pull you up." When he boosted her upright, he swung her into his arms without any more discussion. "You can try a chair if you're sure you're all right." Straightening, he noticed the chaos in his living room for the first time. "Good God! What a mess!"

Paige moaned, seeing the damage. "Oh, no! It looks as if a hurricane had hit it. Do you suppose the rest of the house is as bad?"

"I'll go see." He put her down beside a chair and lingered long enough to shove the cushion back onto it after securing it from the carpet near the fireplace. "Sit down and take it easy while I check."

Paige watched him detour by the brass fireplace tools and select the poker, hefting it in his palm determinedly. "I don't think there's anybody still around," she said in an uneven voice. "At least, I heard the front door close right after I was stuffed in the closet."

"You're probably right—this is just insurance," he said, obviously trying to calm her fears. "I'll be right back."

Paige wasn't aware that she was holding her breath some of the time while he was investigating the rest of the house, but she felt as quivery as a bowl of gelatin when he finally came back into the room and replaced the poker, saying, "All clear. You must have interrupted him just as he was finishing."

"You mean—the whole place is as big a mess?"

" 'Fraid so. It was a pretty thorough search, but I'm damned if I know what he was after."

"I wonder why he didn't take that silver bowl," Paige said, nodding toward a heavy piece at one end of the mantel which was a family favorite. "Or the portable television in the kitchen." She rubbed her forehead fretfully. "What am I talking about television sets for? Are any of your things missing?" She gasped as a sudden thought struck. "Your manuscript?"

He managed a wry grin. "I checked that first thing. Apparently nobody wants the great American novel. There were some pages scattered by the door, but there's nothing missing."

"That must be the new copy I was carrying. It was the reason I came over in the first place; I thought you'd want to check it tonight."

"I wish to hell that you'd waited until morning. . . ."

"That makes two of us." She got up shakily. "What happens now?"

He came over beside her, his brows drawing together as he noted her pale weary face. "First the doctor and then the police, I'd say."

"I don't need a doctor. There's nothing wrong with me that a good night's sleep won't cure." Her hand came up suddenly in alarm. "Do you suppose whoever-it-was went on to Janet's house?"

"I'll go see," Alan said grimly. "You stay here."

"Alone? Not on your life. I'm sticking tight to you."

He started to argue and then took another look at her determined expression. "All right. But you stay on the back porch while I check it out. I don't know why we're quibbling. After all this time, the thief wouldn't still be waiting around."

"You play it your way," she said, going over to pick up the poker he'd discarded, "I'll do it mine."

"In that case—you'd better go first," he said, gesturing her ahead of him down the hall.

His amusement had vanished, however, by the time they reached the outdoor path, and he moved silently ahead of her as they passed the thick shrubbery. Janet's house was still ablaze with lights, Paige noted thankfully when they approached the back door.

"It should be open," she told Alan in a low voice. "I'm sure that I didn't stop to lock it when I left."

"Okay. Wait here," he said, grasping her firmly at either side of her waist and depositing her at the far side of the porch before he started for the door.

"Alan, wait! Take the poker," she hissed, staying on his heels.

"I don't need . . ."

"Please! Otherwise, I'll . . ."

He put a lean hand over her mouth, stopping her in mid-sentence. "If I don't," he soothed in a low voice, "you'll probably use it on me. Hand it over and wait there in the corner. We can fight later."

He disappeared into the house, carrying the poker at his side. It wasn't more than three or four minutes later before he was back, saying, "It's all right. Come on in and lie down. I'd better call the police."

She followed him into the kitchen, noting with amusement that he left the poker casually next to the sink before reaching for the telephone. While he was waiting to be connected, she went on to survey the tidy living room and inspected her bedroom a minute later. The only thing in disarray there was the bedspread, which she'd left partially pulled off the pillows earlier.

She wandered back into the kitchen and found Alan saying, "Right, then. I'll leave things as they are and you can inspect the place in the morning."

He hung up and turned to Page. "The patrol's on short staff tonight. Besides, there's nothing they could check out now that couldn't be done just as well tomorrow."

"You're right about that." She smiled crookedly as she went over to put on the teakettle. "And they're always short-staffed in Cameron Cove. Our big crime wave is on the Fourth of July, when the kids set off cherry bombs at the beach. Hey—what are you doing?"

"Making coffee," he said, pushing her away from the cupboard. "If you won't let me call a doctor, at least go lie on the couch or something."

Since he was treating her so solicitously, Paige decided that she should at least run a comb through her hair. It would be too obvious if she changed from her rumpled jeans at that point, but she could make the best of things.

The minute she peered into the bathroom mirror, she winced visibly. Why on earth hadn't he told her that she'd apparently dusted the closet floor during her enforced stay? And the dirt wasn't only on her blouse; there was a smudge on her cheek as well. When the grime was coupled with her hair standing on end, the net result was God-awful. She uttered an exasperated groan and promptly compounded the felony.

"What's the matter?" Alan's voice sounded on the other side of the bathroom door. "Are you all right in there?"

"Fine. I'm just fine," she blurted in confusion and turned on the water in the basin to drown out any further conversation.

When she entered the living room five minutes later, Alan didn't pursue the matter, simply handing her a mug of coffee as she sank onto the davenport. "You look better," he said finally, sitting in a chair by the fireplace.

Paige translated that to mean she still had a way to go and wasn't surprised that he kept his distance. He'd evidently thrown another log on the fire and brought the blaze to life while she'd been getting cleaned up. As she watched, he took off his tie and shed his tweed sport jacket on the lamp table beside him, but he still looked unfairly alert for that time of night. His shirt was immaculate as usual, and there wasn't a crease in his nicely tailored wool slacks. She noted that as he crossed long legs and made himself comfortable beside the fireplace.

"There are a couple of things I'm wondering about," he said finally in a businesslike tone. "The police asked if you'd ever caught a glimpse of the intruder and I told them no. Was that right?"

She bit her lip, wishing he didn't have to sound quite so much like a public defender just then. Some men might be ladling out a little tenderness; the heroes in those thick books on the end table would have been patting her hand—as well as a lot of other places—and easing her into something sheer and clinging before helping her into bed.

"Well, was it?"

His impatient question showed that sheer and clinging were two adjectives he'd never included in his vocabulary. Paige blinked and said, "I thought I'd made it clear. I don't have the foggiest idea who it was. He was strong . . ."

"He?"

"Well, it was a darned big hand over my face." She considered the idea and nodded. "And tall, I think—but that's all I can remember. It only took about three seconds before the door was locked behind me. It's not much help."

"Maybe it's a good thing that you didn't see any more." When she frowned, he added, "The life span of a good eyewitness can be limited."

She shuddered and put down her coffee mug.

Alan was watching her closely and sat forward in his chair. "Bed for you. If you think of anything else, you can tell the police in the morning."

She chewed her bottom lip as she surveyed him. "Your house is in terrible shape. If you'd like, there's a guest bedroom here to tide you over tonight."

"I can survive in the debris at my place." He kept his voice casual as he said, "Incidentally, I'll check your locks for you before I leave. Apparently there's a mental prisoner loose in this area—he was on a work release program but there's some history of violence in his background."

Her eyes grew wide. "Exactly what kind of violence? I mean, what's he serving time for?"

"Rape and aggravated assault." At her stricken look, Alan tried to sound reassuring. "The authorities are not sure he's even in this area; all they have to go on is an abandoned car."

Paige's imagination couldn't be quelled. "My Lord, it's a good thing I didn't know it when I was in the closet." She got to her feet and faced him determinedly, her pale face giving her a strangely vulnerable air. "Look, I'm sorry to ask a favor like this, but I'd feel a lot better if you'd spend the night here. Otherwise, I'll be worrying about some hardcore crazy climbing the balcony."

"Okay—you don't have to convince me." Alan's slow smile appeared momentarily. "Besides, your guest room sounds a lot better than a night on the couch. I'd better make a quick trip back to my place for a robe and toothbrush. You can lock the door behind me and let me in afterward."

"I'm not quite *that* paranoid yet." She got up and moved a vase on the mantel, taking a key from under it. "This extra door key solves the problem. While you're gone, I'll resurrect an extra pillow—in case you want to read in bed."

"One thing's for sure—there are plenty of books around." His grin lasted longer that time as he nodded toward a lurid paperback that she'd left on the end table after leafing through it earlier.

Paige's chin tilted defensively. "Well, I'm not trying for some practical experience along that line."

"Don't talk like a damned fool!" His gaze flicked

over her derisively before he turned and headed for the door. "I'll be back shortly. In the meantime, you'd better get to bed."

Paige winced as the door slammed behind him. It had not been one of her more intelligent remarks, she decided as she trudged toward the bedroom. Even so, she hadn't wanted him to think . . .

Think what? her conscience berated her. That she'd gotten so carried away by all those amorous story lines that she'd wanted to play, too?

No wonder he'd told her not to be a damned fool, she told herself as she unbuttoned her shirt. She started to hang it in the closet and then dropped it in the bathroom hamper instead. Her reflection in the medicine cabinet mirror didn't help her ego, so she went hurriedly back to the bedroom and shed her jeans. In reaching for a pair of tailored pale yellow pajamas, her fingers hovered over a dainty peach nightgown trimmed in ecru lace which had been a Christmas present. Then, resolutely, she picked up the pajamas. She was only halfway through buttoning the top when she stopped abruptly. It was strange that Alan hadn't mentioned bringing pajamas—just a robe and toothbrush. Not that it mattered, she told herself; she'd just have to be careful about running into him in the hallway.

By the time her robe was securely cinched, she heard a door open. She drew an uncertain breath and then poked her head out into the hall. Alan was bolting the outer door, a paper bag containing his belongings held casually under his arm.

"Everything's all right?" she asked and then grimaced apologetically. "I mean—nothing new?"

"No fiends on the horizon, but we might as well make sure." He checked the bolted door again before coming on down the hall. "I'm glad to see that you decided to be sensible."

For one mad moment, Paige thought he was talking about her severely tailored outfit. Then she realized he meant only that she was going straight to bed. Her pulse rate, which had skyrocketed, settled back down to a sensible beat. "Your room's in here," she said in her best hostess voice as she led him to the twin-bedded room across the hallway from her own. "There's a little view of the cove even though you don't have a balcony."

"It's all right. You don't have to sell me on it," he told her in an amused tone as he dumped the paper bag with his belongings on the nearest bed. "Do we share the bath next door?"

She nodded. "There shouldn't be any problems. I'm all finished with it tonight. If you get hungry, help yourself to anything in the kitchen." Her fingers nervously tightened the belt of her robe again. "I think that's all."

"I'll see you in the morning, then." He put a hand on the edge of his door, ready to close it behind her with unflattering haste. "G'night."

Paige shut her own door an instant later with more firmness than absolutely necessary. There had been no need for him to push her out quite so abruptly, as if he thought she were lingering on the threshold hoping for . . .

For what?

A vision of all the "what" possibilities flickered through her mind with disconcerting clarity.

"Don't be an idiot!" she muttered to herself, and got quickly into bed before she had any more bright ideas.

Alan evidently didn't follow his own prescription, because she heard his door open a little later and his footsteps going toward the living room. At that moment, a vine rustled against her balcony door and she tensed, wondering if there could be someone out there. She debated getting up to investigate but decided against it. The house was securely locked and all she had to do was call to bring Alan running. She let her tense muscles relax and closed her eyes, wondering what he was doing in the living room just then.

The reaction to her ordeal in the closet must have had a more profound effect than she imagined, because she fell into a sound sleep in the midst of her wonderings and didn't even stir for several hours.

Something awakened her just as abruptly, and she sat bolt upright, surprisingly alert. Her bedside alarm showed three a.m. instead of seven, but she still got out of bed, quietly but determinedly. She was starving and there was no use trying to go back to sleep without a detour by the kitchen.

A quick glance into the hallway showed that all was quiet and that Alan had closed his bedroom door before going to sleep. She tiptoed out into the kitchen, deciding to settle for cheese and crackers with a glass of milk. She managed to pour the milk and get the cheese without more than the soft click of the refrigerator door and tucked the cracker box under her arm. It was in turning off the hall light on the way back to her bed that she encountered trouble; the cracker box slipped toward the floor. Trying to catch it would have meant spilling her milk so she muttered a soft "Damn!" and let the box hit her instep. As she bent to retrieve it, Alan's bedroom door flew open and she felt his heavy grip come down on her shoulders, bearing her to the floor.

Her shriek of protest mingled with his "What the hell!" An instant later, he flipped the light switch to discover her sitting in a pool of milk.

"You!" His exclamation was a monument of surprised annoyance.

"Yes, me!" Paige retorted, just as angry. She tried to get to her feet, aware as she made the effort that milk-soaked pajamas apparently stuck like a second skin. "Who in the dickens did you think it was!" she flared, trying to unglue the top when his glance raked over her with masculine thoroughness.

Alan leaned wearily against the wall. "I didn't stop for a questionnaire. Do you have to creep around the place like a family ghost?"

"I didn't want to disturb you." By that time she'd noted that he'd obviously brought a pair of pajamas after all, because some navy blue bottoms were all that he had on.

He translated her wide-eyed appraisal without any embarrassment. "I didn't stop for a robe. Escaped prisoners are inclined to be informal."

She started to rub her forehead and then discovered she was still clutching her empty milk glass. "Next time I'll stomp around in wooden clogs."

A grin transformed his face. "Forget it. I'll clean up this mess while you change. As a matter of fact, I'm hungry, too. Is that the best we can do?" He nodded toward the hunk of cheese on the floor by her bare foot.

"We could have an early breakfast."

"Fair enough. I'll put on a robe," he said, turning toward his room.

"It'll take me a little longer." She was discovering that despite all the virtues of milk baths, the aftermath was decidedly sticky.

Alan lingered long enough to give her a hooded glance over his shoulder. There was a carefully bland expression on his face but a definite hint of amusement in his voice. "Another pair of pajamas like that should be safe enough—in case you're worried about conventions."

"I'm not. And there's nothing wrong with these pajamas."

His gaze roamed deliberately over her again, not missing an inch of her measurements on the way. "I can testify to that. It's amazing what a lot of territory one glass of milk can cover."

It took a hasty shower for Paige to shed the effects of her dunking and to cool her flushed skin. She reappeared in the kitchen in an apricot velveteen hostess wrap with a fitted bodice and swirling skirt, which just happened to be one of the most attractive outfits she possessed. By then, there was only a damp spot on the hall rug as a reminder of her spill, but

Alan looked as disturbing as ever in a navy blue robe which emphasized the breadth of his shoulders.

"Umm, that bacon smells good," she said, going over to inspect the contents of a cast iron frying pan. She stared fixedly at it while searching for something casual to add.

Alan's lips twitched as he noted her concentration. "You'd better be in charge of the toast. I wasn't sure what kind of bread you wanted. Fried eggs all right?"

Paige hesitated on her way to the bread drawer. "Just one egg for me, please. Shall I make coffee?"

"It's already made," he said, nodding toward an electric percolator at the end of the counter as he reached for two plates in the cupboard above him. "Better get cracking on that toast." He shot her a suddenly concerned glance. "You are okay, aren't you?"

"Perfectly. I'm just not functioning on all cylinders yet." She stuffed two pieces of bread in the toaster, trying to move with brisk efficiency.

"I'd never know it. You look pretty damned elegant for this hour. Did you get some sleep earlier on?"

"Uh huh." She kept her attention on the toaster as if the appliance needed her help. "How about you? You were still in the living room the last I heard."

"I wasn't far behind you." He lifted their eggs out of the frying pan with a spatula and turned off the stove burner before carrying their plates over to the breakfast bar, where two places were set. "Actually, I thought I'd read a while, but I almost fell asleep on the first chapter of one of those"—he nodded toward her pile of books at the end of the davenport—"so I decided to go to bed. What's so funny?"

The last came as she started to giggle. "So much for the modern sex novel," she told him, starting to butter the toast. "Maybe there's something wrong with your libido. Of course, there are other logical explanations," she added as his eyebrows climbed.

"Like the possibility that I was tired," he said drily.

"Ummm." She didn't sound convinced as she put two more pieces of bread in the toaster and poured the coffee before sitting down beside him. "Actually, that kind of story is supposed to wake you up."

"Then it must be my libido." For a man who'd just uttered such damning condemnation, he sounded unperturbed. "You can see why I need your help."

"*My* help?" Her fork stopped midway to her lips. "Now just a minute . . ."

". . . with the research," he interrupted, as if she hadn't spoken. "Incidentally, what do you know about fishing?"

"Fishing?" Her voice rose to a squeak.

"You don't have to repeat everything I say," he informed her impatiently. "Why don't you eat your egg before it gets completely cold?"

"Because I like eggs that way," she snapped.

"It's a good thing." He reached for another piece of toast as it emerged from the toaster and started to butter it.

"What about fishing?" she asked, when it was obvious that he wasn't going to say any more.

"I just wanted to know if you were an authority on it, too."

She opened her lips to say "Too?" and then faltered under his stern look. "I know that it's done with a rod and a hook," she managed finally. "My nephew advises bait to go along with it. Does that answer your question?"

His only response was to move her coffee cup further from her reach.

"What's that for?" she wanted to know.

"Obviously, you could use more sleep and coffee won't help. That's what happens when you lose your temper," he added as she yanked the cup back and spilled a good part into the saucer in the process. "Don't try anything foolish," he went on as she hefted the cup and eyed him narrowly. "You should know by now that I'm lacking in most gentlemanly instincts. Another symptom of my defective libido."

Paige smiled despite herself and got up to drain her saucer in the sink before sitting down again. "What's with this fishing bit?" she asked, putting some jelly on her toast and taking a bite.

"It's my friend, George," Alan said in a resigned tone. "That's his aim in life while he's down here. I'd like to keep him happy, so he's going to appear at the crack of dawn to go fishing with me."

"You sound as if you'd made a date for the electric chair. Lots of people like fishing."

"If I had some extra time, I'd feel the same

way." He looked grim. "Unfortunately, I signed a contract to deliver that miserable novel."

"From what I typed, it sounds like a great novel."

"It would be better with an ending," he said, putting down his fork and pushing his empty plate aside. "I hadn't planned on keeping George company while I was down here. That's why I thought you . . ."

". . . could do it instead? I'm sorry. I know even less about fishing than I do about sex." Too late, she realized where her unwary tongue had led her. "The kind they write about in novels, I mean."

"Of course."

He stared back at her, making no attempt to hide a thoughtful, obviously calculating expression. She felt herself flush and experienced an unholy desire to strike back. "There's always your brunette," she said in a testy tone. When he scowled, puzzled, she went on, "The woman you were with all day yesterday. Thor saw you leaving the Conquistador."

"Oh, you mean Barb." Enlightenment chased his scowl away. In fact, even a mention of the woman seemed to put him in good humor, Paige thought. It didn't help her own disposition when he added, "She's too busy."

But apparently not too busy for a lunch date, Paige could have told him. Instead she said, "Thor's busy, too, but he might take over for you. He owes me a favor or two."

Alan's scowl reappeared. "George's hangover was monumental after their initial encounter. I'd just as soon he didn't try to drink your friend Thor under the table another time."

"In that case your best bet is to drop him off in Depoe Bay with one of the charter captains and tell them to leave the beer on shore. The only other person I know who'd make sure he stayed sober would be Liza."

"Does she know anything about fishing?"

"Of course." Paige smiled reminiscently. "She took it up for a hobby one summer. The next year she concentrated on golf. Right now, it's hooked rugs."

"You're sure she can catch fish?"

Paige nodded. "She claims it only needs a scientific approach. My theory is that the fish don't dare ignore her hook."

"Can you get in touch with her first thing in the morning?"

"Yes, of course. I'll set the alarm to make sure I wake up," she said, getting to her feet and going to the sink to rinse off her plate.

"Don't bother with that. I'll clean this up," Alan said as he came over beside her.

"In that case, I'll go to bed." The words came out jerkily despite all her efforts to sound casual. She started to turn away but found herself brought up short. It wasn't surprising; Alan had caught the belt of her robe, and, other than indulging in a wrestling match that she was slated to lose, she had to stand there under his scrutiny. "Did you want something else?" she managed to ask.

His shoulders shook with laughter. "My dear girl,

you don't have to flinch every time I get within six feet."

"I'm not your dear girl—or your anything. And it's too late or too early to play games." She glared up at him. "I should have known that you'd—" Too late she saw where she was heading and her voice trailed off.

"Go on, finish your sentence. You should have known that I'd what?" There wasn't any amusement in his gray eyes now; they were more the color of the storm clouds that had hovered all day. When she kept her lips obstinately closed, he went on, "Take advantage of spending the night here? Is that what's worrying you?"

"I'm not sure." She stared defiantly at a point three inches over the top of his broad shoulder. "Anyhow, I told you not to get any wrong ideas."

"For God's sake, sharing the same kitchen and living room doesn't mean that we have to share the same bed." He dropped the belt of her robe as if it had turned red hot. "Maybe it was a mistake to have you read all of that purple prose. Next thing you'll be imagining that the meter reader is lusting for you."

She drew herself up stiffly. "I don't have to stand here and listen to such drivel."

"Oh, yes, you do." A strong hand clamped down on her shoulder when she tried to turn away. "All I had in mind was telling you to skip setting your alarm in the morning. I'll have to be up to talk to the police when they arrive at the annex and I was going to knock on your door when I left. So you can set that imagination of yours to rest. I have better things to do."

"Than humor your frustrated secretary? Is that what you were going to say?"

"Damned if you're not asking for it!" he growled, and instead of releasing her, his hand slid deliberately down to where her robe's V-neckline ended in the soft, shadowed valley between her breasts. As she gasped in surprise, he caught at the edges of the robe and twisted them, grinding his knuckles against her skin as he pulled her even closer.

She stood rigid in his grasp, as if unable to believe what was happening and, at the same time, trying to ignore the flood of awareness between them. She knew instantly that she was beyond her depth—that she was being submerged by waves of feeling so tantalizing that it was painful to resist. What she really wanted to do was follow Alan's lead—mold herself to him and pull his head down so his lips could cover hers. Only the knowledge that he expected such a capitulation made her hesitate.

Evidently that was something Alan hadn't anticipated. "You don't have to act the innocent any longer," he said in a rough, uneven tone. "From now on, we're just two consenting adults. I had a feeling that we'd arrive at this point the first time I saw you. If you're honest, you'll admit it's what you were angling for, too."

His reasoning was so painfully close to the truth that it was all Paige needed to break the spell between them. She wrenched furiously away from him as she gritted out, "Take your hands off me! I'm not angling for anything from you!"

She got halfway down the hall toward her bedroom before she looked over her shoulder to see him staring dispassionately after her. He gestured as her gaze met his. "Go on to bed. That was a very nice exit line, so you'd better quit while you're ahead."

She rounded on him at the threshold of her room. "Look—just stay away from me. That's all I ask."

"Whatever you say." In contrast to her outburst of temper, he sounded bored by the whole affair. "You're strictly off-limits from now on so far as I'm concerned. Just get the typing done and call that assistant of yours to take care of George in the morning."

"So long as it only involves fishing . . ."

He stared at her, his lips tight. "What in the hell are you imagining now?"

"Just some of the things that happen between two consenting adults."

Her saccharine mimicry of his previous words made him grimace. "Touché. I gather that Liza is another one who believes in 'I do' before 'I will'?"

"Is that a crime?" Paige said with cool dignity. "Not all women play musical beds—despite what you read in the papers, Mr. Bayne. Liza can show your friend where to catch fish, but if he makes one wrong move, she'll use him for bait. I forgot to mention that judo is another hobby of hers."

"I'll tell George," Alan said drily. "It might be better if he took up another hobby. On the other hand, it's just possible that he's only interested in fishing, so she can leave her black belt at home. Are there any other pearls of wisdom that you have to impart before we cut this conversation short?"

"Not especially." She waved toward the remnants of their meal on the counter. "I'd rather you left the cleaning up."

His jaw firmed. "I said I'd take care of it and I will. Why all the fuss?"

"Because you should use soap instead of detergent in the cast iron frying pan. Otherwise you'll ruin the finish." As she saw his eyes close in resignation, she hurried on, "It might not sound important to you . . ."

"You're right. It doesn't." He tightened the belt on his robe and took one step toward where she was hovering in her bedroom doorway. "If you have any more brilliant instructions—damned if you won't find yourself stuffed in another closet. Go to bed!" He watched her pale cheeks flare with color as she drew in an aggrieved breath and then whirled into her bedroom.

Alan's angry expression faded as he stood looking at her closed door. Then, in a gesture of weary frustration, he smashed his fist against his palm and strode back to the kitchen.

Chapter Five

There was light edging the drapes at the balcony window when Paige opened her eyes a few hours later. She was so exhausted she would have immediately gone back to sleep if another knock hadn't sounded on her bedroom door. "Who is it?" she wanted to know, pushing up on an elbow.

"Now who do you think?" Alan's voice sounded crisp, even from the hall. "Are you going to get up?"

Paige squinted at the clock and rolled out of bed. She managed to get one arm in her terry cloth robe before opening the door and found him, fully dressed, with his hand poised to knock again. "What's going on?" she asked, trying to pull herself together. "Is anything wrong?"

"It depends on your point of view. There's a policeman waiting to talk to you in the living room of the annex."

"Oh, Lord," she groaned, "why didn't you wake me up?"

"I just did." He rubbed the back of his neck, showing that despite being shaved and dressed in clean cotton slacks and sport shirt, his own lack of sleep was making itself felt. "I left coffee on the stove. Since there isn't a rash of crime in Cameron Cove, it won't hurt the chief to wait a little longer. Incidentally, George is due within the hour, so . . ."

". . . I'd better call Liza." Just then Paige felt more like tearing her hair out than combing it. Alan's uncompromising expression showed that he hadn't forgotten their altercation earlier, and his initial appraisal of her appearance—heavy-eyed and clad in her worn terry robe—probably had him thanking his stars that he hadn't gotten more involved last night. Every syllable he'd uttered showed that there wouldn't be any trouble keeping her at arm's length from now on. His next sentence confirmed it.

"I'm sorry that we had words last night. I should have remembered that you were almost in shock when I found you earlier. The sensible thing would have been to call the doctor."

"That's ridiculous. There was nothing wrong with me."

"Maybe nothing serious, but you were fair game for an attack of nerves. I didn't help by sticking around." He shoved his hands in his pockets, still keeping a safe distance. "Probably you'd have fared better with the fiend."

"Oh, for heaven's sake! You don't have to take all the blame." Paige pulled the collar of her robe tighter, mainly to have something to do. "I lost my temper, too."

"Okay. So we've both said our piece—now we can forget it." He turned back down the hall. "I'll waiting in the annex with the chief."

"I won't be long."

After he'd gone, Paige headed resolutely for the shower, despite a yearning to bury her head under the nearest pillow. How diplomatic of Alan to lay all the trouble to an attack of nerves—ignoring terms like mutual attraction and propinquity and awareness and desire. It was like calling a volcanic eruption a slight geologic disturbance, she decided, and gasped as she turned on the cold water to take her mind off that dangerous track.

Liza wasn't enthusiastic about her new assignment when Paige called her ten minutes later after scrambling into a pair of trim-fitting wool slacks and a chamois shirt.

"Are you serious?" was the other's first question. "I'm supposed to transcribe the notes for the Chamber of Commerce meeting this morning and run off copies of their newsletter afterward. I always do that on Tuesday."

"Surely it won't matter if the newsletter is a little late. When's their next meeting?"

"Next month, but they're one of our best accounts."

"Look, I'm not suggesting a trip to the Antarctic. All you have to do is take a man fishing this forenoon. Maybe buy him lunch afterwards."

"It sounds funny to me. Are you sure he wants a woman for a fishing guide?"

"What does that have to do with it?" Paige answered evasively. "It's a free fishing trip. He'd be crazy to object."

Liza's snort of laughter came clearly over the telephone wire. "Where have you been for the last twenty years? Most men don't even want a woman along—let alone one telling them where to go."

"Look, Liza! You don't tell him that—you merely guide him politely and make sure he comes home with some fish."

"The safest way to do that is stop by the CrabSpot," the other said, naming the Cove's best fish market.

"That's up to you. I'd just look on it as another job. Only this one's in the fresh air."

"You're the boss—although what your sister would say . . ."

"Don't worry about Janet," Paige cut in. "I'll explain to her when she comes home. Get over here as fast as you can, will you? If I don't answer the door, come on to the annex."

"At this hour of the morning? I must say, you keep long hours for that man."

Paige started to explain that she was really going to see the chief of police but decided against it. Things were confused enough already. "I do, don't I?" she managed brightly, and hung up before Liza could ask any more questions.

The chief of police was perched on the edge of the davenport in the annex, coffee mug in hand, watching Alan reassemble pages of manuscript at the table nearby, when Paige knocked and walked in.

The officer was a middle-aged, lanky individual with an intelligent face and searching blue eyes, a far cry from the redneck types that Hollywood delighted in casting as small town policemen. Paige remembered meeting him at a community club meeting from a previous summer and reminded him of it when Alan would have introduced them.

"Although this is actually the first time I've met you in an official capacity," she said to the officer as he stood to greet her.

"Let's hope it's the last time," Chief Sherwood retorted, sitting on the davenport again after she subsided on a fireplace bench. "I'm sorry to get you up so early. Especially since Mr. Bayne says that you can't provide much actual description."

"Practically nothing," Paige agreed. "This figure loomed up and two seconds later I was shoved into a closet and the door was being locked behind me. If I'd known that there was an escaped mental patient in the neighborhood, I'd have really been a gibbering idiot by the time Alan—er, Mr. Bayne—found me."

The Chief looked startled but nodded, waiting for Alan to emerge from the kitchen and give her a mug of coffee before saying, "Then there's nothing you can add to the physical description?"

"Not now." Paige kept her glance averted from Alan, who lingered by the fireplace, as she went on. "It seemed like an awfully big hand, if that's any help."

"What kind of skin?" When she frowned uncomprehendingly, the chief added, "Calloused? A working man's hand? Was it a sweater sleeve or shirt cuff? Can you remember anything like that?"

"Oh, Lord." Paige compressed her lips as she thought about it and then shook her head again. "I can't say for sure. Right now, nothing's very clear. It happened so fast," she said apologetically, "I didn't even really get scared until afterward."

"Well, think about it for a while and call me if anything surfaces," the law officer said, putting his coffee mug on the end table and getting to his feet. "In the meantime," he said, looking across at Alan, "it wouldn't hurt to keep your doors and windows locked. I'm still wondering why this is the only place that was ransacked. Usually there's a definite pattern for break-ins. Of course, the intruder may have thought the place was between rentals."

"He knows different now, so let's hope he'll go south for the rest of the winter," Alan said. "At least Paige interrupted him before he could make off with any valuables."

"You mean there's nothing missing?" she asked in amazement.

"Not that I can see," he replied coolly. "You might check your household inventory before you start typing."

"I'll be on my way," Chief Sherwood said, retrieving his uniform cap from the hall table and starting for the front door. "Nice to have talked to you again, Miss Kendall. Let's hope the rest of your stay at the Cove is more peaceful."

Alan saw the policeman out and came back to find her checking the page numbers of typescript on the table where she'd worked the day before. "Everything seems to be here," she said unnecessarily, since she was sure that he was very much aware of it. "I don't think I'll have to do more than two or three pages over—the ones that are so creased."

"There's plenty of time for that. You'd better have some breakfast first. I'd offer to make you some but . . ."

"I wouldn't think of it," she interrupted, trying to sound brisk. "There's scads of food at home, so I don't need to bother you. Thanks just the same."

"It isn't any bother. If you'd let me finish, I was going to say that I didn't get to a grocery yesterday so my cupboard's pretty bare." He gestured toward the kitchen behind him.

There was only one possible response to that. "Of course, you're very welcome to have something at my house. There's plenty in the refrigerator."

"No, thanks." He slouched against the wall and let her have his full attention. "I'd better stick around to be on hand when George arrives."

Paige glanced at her watch, trying to ignore the obvious slight he'd dealt. All he had to do was leave a note on the front door and tell George where to find him. Which meant that Alan didn't want to face her across the breakfast table, either. Since that was exactly the way she felt, the fact shouldn't have hurt. Unfortunately, it did. She tried to mask it, saying lightly, "Are you sure George won't be too unhappy with your change in plans? Liza thought he might."

"But she's still coming?"

Paige nodded. "She hoped that he didn't have a built-in male prejudice against women fishing guides."

"I'd say that depended just as much on her attitude as his. But maybe that's my male chauvinism." Alan straightened and walked over to open the front door. "I'll bring George over when he arrives."

The bout of verbal fencing didn't improve Paige's appetite. When she got home again, she found that toast and coffee were the only things that sound bearable and, after half a piece of toast, decided to take two aspirin for the headache she'd suddenly developed.

Liza arrived soon afterward, exuding vim and vigor in every movement. "What's the matter with you?" she wanted to know, casting a keen glance toward Paige as they trudged back to the kitchen. "Most people look better after a few days at the ocean; you're going downhill."

"That's all I needed to make my day." Paige gestured toward the percolator. "Have some coffee."

"No, thanks. Maybe that's your trouble—too much coffee, I mean. Have you tried yogurt instead?"

Paige gave her a bleak look across the kitchen. "Nope. I haven't tried strangling anybody at the breakfast table, either, but I may start any minute."

Liza's eyebrows shot up but her prim features softened as she said, "That's what happens when I get on a reform jag. You and Janet are the only ones who aren't afraid to tell me off now and then."

"That's all right. I'm not exactly a ray of sunshine

today, either." Paige leaned her chin on her palm and tried to ignore the pounding in her head. "I didn't get enough sleep. Did you know there's an escaped mental patient in the neighborhood?"

"It's not the first time." Liza unzipped her rainproof jacket before perching on a kitchen stool. "You surely didn't stay awake worrying about that?"

"Not really." Suddenly it seemed too much work for lengthy explanations. "Probably I'm not used to a strange bed. Can you use your car today? I don't know whether George—" Paige paused, trying to remember the man's last name. She couldn't go through life calling him "old George." The way things were, Alan would probably leave the introductions up to her, and how in the deuce would she cope with that?

"What's the matter? Don't you feel well?" Liza asked, concerned.

"Sorry. I didn't mean to go off in a fog. I couldn't remember your fisherman's last name."

"Is that all?" Liza shrugged and slipped off her jacket. She looked much trimmer than usual in jeans that were the right size and a blue flannel shirt which had apparently shrunk in the wash, emerging almost whistle-bait. "Things are informal on a fishing trip. I'll just call him George and he can call me . . ."

". . . Miss Strom." Paige bit her lip to hide outright laughter. "Not the way you look this morning. He'll be lucky if he can keep his mind on the fish."

"That's ridiculous." Liza reverted to her usual astringent self. "Who is the man, anyhow?"

"A friend of Alan Bayne's. That's all I know—" Paige broke off as the back doorbell sounded. "Here they are now."

She went over to open the door and found Alan with another man waiting on the porch. Her first glance told her that "old George" had been misnamed. He couldn't have been much more than forty, and, although he was stockily built, with slightly thinning fair hair that was gray at the temples, he had alert blue eyes behind horn-rimmed glasses. Catching her glance on him, he flashed a cheerful grin that made her smile in return.

"Paige, this is George Porter," Alan said immediately, as she ushered them into the room. "Paige Kendall. And Miss Strom over there in the corner," he continued with a quiet courtesy that brought an involuntary smile from the secretary.

"Liza," she said automatically, and then looked confused at hearing the words come out.

"Liza it is," George said, going over to vigorously shake hands with her. "Alan said how busy you were, so I think it's great that you're willing to take the time to go out with me. There's nothing like having a guide who knows the ropes. Can we rent gear where we're going? Thor offered his but I didn't take him up on it. You know Thor Goransen, don't you? The fellow down at the hotel?"

"I know him."

Liza's flat tone should have put the man off but he

ignored it, telling her confidentially, "I don't think he takes fishing seriously."

"He doesn't take anything seriously—except having a good time."

"That isn't quite true," Paige said, feeling she should stick up for Thor in his absence. "Actually, he works hard at his job most of the time."

"I'm sure he'd appreciate your testimonial," Alan said, sounding bored by the whole discussion. "But I know George is aching to get started, so if Liza's ready . . ."

"Any time." Liza reached for her jacket and looked surprised when George lingered to help her into her. "My car's out in front. I'm not sure when we'll be back," she told Paige. "I put the office on the answering machine. You'd better check for calls later."

"I will." Paige smiled at both of them as she opened the door. "Have a great time. If you catch a whopper, I'll start reading the fish section of my cookbook."

"We'll take you up on that." George looked like a man who'd discovered that Christmas had arrived early. He was fairly bouncing with enthusiasm but remembered to help Liza down the steps.

His unexpected gallantry surprised the secretary so much that she almost took a header into the shrubbery when he tucked a hand at her elbow. Fortunately the reason for it passed him by. "My dear, are you all right?" he inquired solicitously.

"Fine." She sounded dazed, but Paige noticed that she didn't dislodge his helping hand.

After they'd driven off, Paige followed Alan back into the kitchen, saying, "He's nice," in some surprise.

"Don't be so amazed." Alan leaned against the end of the counter to survey her dispassionately. "What did you expect? The latest model with horns?"

"You just said he was a friend of yours." She stopped abruptly as she realized that it wasn't the most diplomatic comment she could have made.

Naturally, Alan didn't let it pass, either. "I haven't known him long, so he hasn't had much chance to be corrupted."

"That wasn't what I meant at all," Paige said irritably, wondering why he seemed determined to be disagreeable. "I was just surprised that he had such beautiful manners."

Alan folded his arms across his chest. "And that warms female hearts?"

"I don't know about that," she retorted, just as sarcastically.

"You're supposed to, by now. I thought that's what you were checking out for me." He gestured toward the pile of books on the end table, which she hadn't touched since depositing them there the day before. "That's the whole point of the exercise."

"Not according to your instructions. You wanted to know about all the sexy passages," she told him indignantly.

"So that I could find out what appealed to feminine readers. What in the devil have you been doing with your time?"

"Checking out the sexy passages," she said, not yielding one inch. "I even made up a chart."

"About what?"

"What they did. What the characters talked about. The kind of descriptions." She gestured as she ran out of words. "You know what I mean."

"I wish I did." He stayed at the end of the counter and looked down his nose at her, obviously unimpressed. "You'd better get your notes."

She shot him a suspicious glance to see if he meant it, wishing that she was in better shape to cope with his annoyance. The aspirin hadn't helped, and she would have liked to lie on the couch and hide under the mohair comforter. Which meant that a psychiatrist could have a field day with her, she decided as she searched through some papers on the end table. She finally found her shorthand notebook under the tide table, the weekly television schedule, and a stray chocolate chip cookie.

Alan didn't miss that, either. "I hope note-taking didn't interfere with your other tasks," he said, sounding thoroughly disagreeable.

"Next time I'll store the list in a locked drawer," she said, brushing her hair back before ruffling through the pages. "Where do you want me to start?"

He waved negligently.

Just as if he were an Indian potentate, she thought angrily. Somebody should tell him they'd gone out with the Empire years before. She focused on a page with an effort and read aloud, "Blend the sugar and the shortening," stopping abruptly at his annoyed growl.

"Is that a recipe for an aphrodisiac?" he wanted to know.

She wondered frantically if she could add a pinch of rhinoceros horn and a teaspoon of ginseng to carry it off. Seeing his brooding expression, she decided against it. "Actually it's pound cake," she admitted. "I can't imagine how it got in there."

Alan made a production out of looking at his watch. "Could we get on?"

"Whatever you say." She'd found her place by then. "Would you like to start with locale?"

"What kind of locale?"

"For the most passionate passages," she said, trying to sound businesslike.

"I presume that would be a bed."

"You're wrong about that. Two hearth rugs, one gravel beach, and one—er, lay—in the heather. The last was in Scotland."

"I didn't think it was the Bronx." He sounded amused, despite himself. "Go on."

She kept her eyes on her notebook. "There was another interlude on horseback. I wasn't quite sure how they managed." She kept her expression solemn, finally staring across at him. "If you'd like me to find the chapter, I could read it aloud."

"Never mind, it would be safer to avoid the horseback bit." He stared at her fixedly. "You're sure it was a gravel beach? In that other book?"

"Oh, yes. I think the heroine wore a cloak."

"I'm glad."

When the silence lengthened after his dry comment, she turned a page in her notebook and read on. "The time sequences were interesting, too. Apparently the—er—passionate love—"

"I know what you mean. There is a word for it."

"Several." Her glance stayed down. "The passionate love scenes came at very strange times. Once when the heroine was pulled out of the lake. The hero had to warm her afterward to combat the freezing temperatures."

"Practically medicinal."

"Unique would be a better word. The hero used his own body to warm her. I think the exact phrase was 'covered her like a blanket' for most of the forenoon."

"Did she suffer from exposure?"

"No, but"—Paige pursed her lips as she tried to think—"but he caught pneumonia and died ten pages later. The heroine gave birth to twins in the last chapter, on her way to the New World."

"You're making this up."

"Scout's honor." She consulted her notebook again. "The passionate love scene on the bearskin rug in front of the fireplace came because . . ."

"Let me guess. The heroine was suffering from too much heat."

"In more ways than one," Paige said primly. "The horseback interval came in the desert."

"My hero doesn't get out of the mountains."

"There are always pack horses . . ."

"We'll skip that angle," Alan said firmly. "Now, let's see if I have this right. The best time for," he paused as Paige cleared her throat warningly, and then went on, "the best time for the passionate love scenes comes at odd hours in the most unlikely place imaginable—whenever there's a plausible reason for the heroine to shed her clothes." He shot Paige a thoughtful glance. "I presume the hero helps in that maneuver."

She nodded, checking her list again. "For about three pages. First she resists him but she's eventually overcome. Mostly after she feels his hands on—"

"Yes?" Alan's voice was bland as she paused and blushed.

"On her breasts. And other intimate parts. I didn't know there were so many intimate parts," she added almost resentfully. "By now, I could write an anatomy book."

"That's not the market I'm after."

"You know what I mean," she said, frowning across at him.

"I don't understand why you're so unhappy about it. You're supposed to feel aroused, titillated, excited. . . ."

"I'm excited by hot fudge sundaes, too," she told him levelly. "After an afternoon of them, I'm sick to my stomach."

His lips twitched but he kept his tone solemn. "There must be a moral to this somewhere."

Paige hadn't missed that fleeting glimmer of amusement. She closed her shorthand book with a snap. "Not necessarily. Morals were the one thing I *didn't* find," she said, deliberately misunderstanding him. "Is that enough information for you?"

He appeared to consider it. "Under ordinary circumstances, I'd say yes. But I could use a little more in the contemporary genre. Skip the historicals to concentrate on adventure stories and westerns."

"I thought the hero kissed the horse in the western. Just before they rode off into the sunset."

Alan's eyebrows rose. "Obviously you're misinformed. Try to approach the new material without prejudice. Otherwise, the whole thing's a waste of time." He frowned suddenly as she muttered something succinct. "What did you say?"

"I said 'damn.' Because I broke the point of my pencil."

"You don't have a pencil."

"I did yesterday. That's when I broke it. I just remembered."

His eyes narrowed. "If you don't like the job, I can always make other arrangements."

Paige recalled the balance in her bank account and swallowed the retort she wanted to make. "I'll be glad to do some more research," she said finally, with an effort. "Of course, I'll have to buy some more books."

He reached for his wallet and pulled out two twenty-dollar bills. "That should make a start. Can you get on it today?"

"I suppose so. Unless you'd rather I spent more time typing your manuscript. When did you say it was due at the publisher's?"

"Too damned soon." He rubbed his face with his palm. "Just keep to the schedule we set up. I should be back by dinner time to check with you."

"I didn't know you were leaving," she faltered.

"There's still some unfinished business in Portland. When George comes back, he'll probably stay with me at the annex. At least he will if he has any sense."

The last came in a bitter undertone that brought Paige's head up sharply. "Why? Is there some reason that he shouldn't be alone?"

"Nothing serious." Alan's tone was casual, almost elaborately so. "The man's just been overworking."

"Was that why he tried to drink Thor under the table?"

"Probably. It's the reason I'm encouraging fishing trips with Liza instead of get-togethers with the boys. I'd appreciate your assistance along that line."

She surveyed him intently. "You don't look like a demon chaperone. Or the big brother type either."

"I'm surprised that something has escaped that searching eye of yours. Do I detect a note of approval?"

"It's immaterial to me one way or the other," she said, priding herself on her tone.

"Just another job?" he probed.

"I wish you'd stop putting words in my mouth," she complained. "But if you must know, that's it in a nutshell."

"Which shows that I haven't organized my tactics as well as the heroes in that bunch of fluff," he said, jerking his head again toward the pile of books on the table.

She pretended to think. "As I recall, the leading men didn't worry about such things. They were charming and gallant."

"Everything a woman could hope for," he said, finishing her sentence again as she paused. He reached out and pulled her close to him. "I'd hate to think that I'd let the side down."

"Don't be ridiculous," she snapped, wishing that she'd more sense than to deliberately taunt the man. She didn't attempt to hold his glance as he stared down at her. He had the ability to see far too much and the last thing she wanted at that moment was to have her mind read. Forcing herself to remain stiff and unyielding in his clasp, she said, "I don't know what you have in mind but—"

The telephone rang, cutting her words off decisively. For an instant, they stood without moving, the air heavy with tension between them. Then Alan brought his hand up and carefully fastened the top button on her shirt, which had worked open when he'd yanked her against him. "There you are," he said with a smile that didn't have a particle of humor in it. "All neat and tidy again. I don't know when I've met anybody quite so—" As he searched for an adjective, the telephone rang again. "You'd better answer that while you have the chance," he told her, dropping his arms to his sides.

Paige tried to look as if she didn't care one way or the other when she went over to pick up the receiver. She could feel the warmth in her cheeks and knew that Alan had a very good idea that her heartbeat was thundering away. Probably he'd even felt it when he'd buttoned her blouse. Her skin still burned from his touch.

"Hello, Paige, is that you?"

The familiar voice over the wire brought her thoughts abruptly back to the present. "Thor. What got you up so early?" Behind her, she heard Alan give an annoyed mutter, and she tried for even more enthusiasm in her voice. "Have you had breakfast yet?"

"Of course I have," Thor's deep voice reverberated. "You don't have a monopoly on the sunrise, love. I'm calling about lunch."

She managed to look suitably anxious as she turned toward Alan, repeating, "Lunch? Today?"

"Tell him you have to work," Alan said impatiently, looking at his watch.

"Is there somebody with you?" Thor sounded equally disgruntled. "What kind of hours does that guy keep, for God's sake?"

Paige knew better than to answer that. "I'd better call you back, Thor."

"Don't bother. I'm leaving," Alan said. "But I expect to have another chapter to check when I get back. Remember that if your chum suggests a two-hour lunch."

As a tender farewell, Paige realized it fell decidedly short. She tried not to show her disappointment once the kitchen door closed behind him. "I'm sorry about that," she told Thor, trying to remember if she'd kept her hand over the mouthpiece at the critical time. "Mr. Bayne was just leaving."

"So I heard. I didn't know you could get away with talking to a secretary that way these days. Why don't you tell him off? If you need some extra cash, I could help you out."

"It's not that. Janet made the arrangements before I arrived, so the least I can do is follow through. Besides," she added with a twinge of conscience, "he's not usually that dictatorial. We had a slight disagreement."

Thor's guffaw shattered her attempt to be tactful. "I'll bet. From the way he sounded, you'd left him on the ropes. I have an idea—why don't you sic Liza on him?"

"I can't. She's busy keeping old George happy. They're on a fishing trip."

"You're kidding!"

"No, I'm not. What's so strange about that?"

"If you don't know, I'm not about to tell you. I'll reserve a place at the bar for him tonight. He'll need it after spending the day with her."

"That's ridiculous. Liza can be perfectly charming. You're just prejudiced."

"With damn good reason," he cut in. "Why waste time discussing it? If you want to fight for women's rights, we can do it at lunch."

"Okay. Besides, I'm too tired to fight any more this morning," she confessed.

"Don't you feel well?"

"It was a long night," she temporized. "Did you know there's an escaped mental patient wandering around the neighborhood?"

"That doesn't surprise me. I think four of his friends just registered from Los Angeles."

"Thor, I'm serious."

"So am I; you should see these creeps. On the other hand, you probably will—at lunch. If they find their way out of the bar. Maybe we should eat at another hotel."

"You heard what my boss said. No long lunches."

"The hell with his ultimatums! You have to eat. What's the difference between a sandwich at home or a free lunch here at the Conquistador?"

Paige let herself be convinced. "But it will have to be a fast one."

"Fair enough. Knock on my door when you come. I don't have anything vital on my schedule today."

"You're sure?" she asked, loath to take advantage of his good nature. "No lovely, rich tourists crossing the threshold?"

"Not that you'd notice."

The acid in his voice made her hastily change the subject. "All right. I'll see you around noon. And thanks, Thor."

"No trouble," he said with rare understanding. "We can weep on each other's shoulders."

"And keep a watchful eye on your four fruitcakes from southern California?"

"Who? Oh, them! I'm running a check on their credit now, so they may not still be around."

"You're beginning to sound like Scrooge these days."

"It's about time," he said grimly. "I've been a slow learner. According to our accountant, a little too slow. At the moment, we're hanging on by our fingernails, so I can't make many more mistakes and still keep the Conquistador."

"If things are that bad, you shouldn't be buying my lunch," she responded, concerned at his news.

He broke out laughing. "I'm talking about thousands of dollars, Paige love. My bank balance can still handle some champagne and caviar, so let's not have any more of that nonsense. As a matter of fact, I'm counting on an unexpected dividend this month, so you can even have dessert."

"Fair enough. I'll order from the left side of the menu," she said, adopting his tone. "And I'll try to make it by twelve-thirty."

Once she'd hung up, she went back to the bedroom to change her clothes, unwilling to appear at the Conquistador in what she had on. She pulled out a dress in sunny shades of orange with a white tucked bib bodice. The bright colors were a morale booster on another morning where the predominant shade outside was gray. Apparently spring was making only rare appearances from behind winter's skirts.

Paige was enough of a realist to wear a raincoat when she headed for the office a little later. To soothe her conscience, she told herself that she'd go shopping for another armful of books after she'd lunched with Thor. In the meantime, she owed it to Janet to make sure that the office was still functioning properly while Liza was on her special assignment.

Fortunately, their steady customers who'd left messages didn't have anything pressing—one of the joys of living at Cameron Cove. In a city, those requests would have been demands, and the deadlines would have been yesterday rather than "whenever it's convenient." Even so, the time slipped away faster than she'd planned and it was after noon before she left for the Conquistador.

Thor was standing behind the reception desk when she arrived. He was moodily thumbing through a ledger that apparently didn't have as many reservations as he would have preferred, but he managed a smile. "That's my girl—right on time. I hope you're hungry."

"There's nothing to improve my appetite like the prospect of a free lunch," she told him solemnly.

"Help! There goes the profit for the month." He tossed the ledger aside and came around the end of the counter. "At least you're honest about it, which is more than I can say for some of the women around here."

As they waited for the elevator to take them to the top-floor dining room, she surveyed him with amusement. "Stop being so grouchy. Didn't you have enough sleep either?"

"Does anybody?" He followed her into the elevator and pushed the top button. "At least I had sense enough not to risk getting seasick, too." He gestured her ahead of him off the elevator and into the sparsely tenanted dining room, waving aside the hostess and showing Paige to a window table himself. "I'd already arranged a charter for my cruiser," he said, sitting across from her. "It was too late to change plans just to accommodate George. I'm surprised that he went off in a huff, though. Oh well, there'll be other days."

"I don't think he was upset about anything. At least he didn't look it when I saw him." Paige was perusing the menu carefully. "Umm—everything looks good. Will my credit run to chowder and a shrimp louie?"

Thor waved that aside, giving the order tersely to the waitress who paused by their table. "I'll have the same," he told her. "Bring some water—it should have been here before this."

The girl flushed at his tone and hurried off, returning promptly to fill their glasses. "I'm sorry, Mr. Goransen. Is there anything else?"

"Just what I told you. Preferably in order. And that twosome by the window wants their check." After the waitress moved off, he turned to Paige, saying, "She won't last."

"I suppose it is hard to get trained dining room staff."

"Or trained anything else. The one good thing about a bad month is that the next one's usually better." He let his glance wander over her and said, "You don't look as if anything's bothering you. I should pay you to stick around and improve the decor."

"I'm enjoying playing hooky for the moment. It does wonders for the morale."

"That boss of yours could wear anybody down." A sudden grin creased Thor's good-looking features. "Just like Liza. Poor old George—imagine having to put up with her and the remains of a hangover, too. He'll be a stretcher case by the time he gets back tonight."

"Don't be too sure. They were getting along fine the last I saw."

"Are we talking about the same people? Li'l Liza,

the community conscience? Purveyor of rules for all the two-legged occupants of Cameron Cove and probably the four-legged ones, too? Somebody said she was getting up a petition for an animal neutering clinic. It's right up her alley."

Paige was glad their meal arrived at that moment. While she didn't want to alienate Thor, she wasn't disposed to let him criticize Liza in such a one-sided fashion. "This looks marvelous," she said, smiling her thanks at the waitress when she brought the chowder and a rattan basket of oyster crackers to go with it. "I'd forgotten how good really fresh seafood is," she went on to Thor when they were alone again. "After eating all this, I'll probably fall asleep over my work this afternoon."

"I thought Bayne was supposed to be a pretty good writer," Thor said, crumbling a cracker on top of his chowder.

Paige had no intention of admitting that it wasn't Alan's manuscript that was apt to send her nodding but the stack of new books she still had to buy. "He doesn't talk about his work very much. It surprised me. I thought he'd be the great 'literary genius' type."

"He's hardly a shrinking violet," Thor pointed out.

"You can say that again." Her lips thinned, as if she'd suddenly discovered a particle of sand in the last bite of clam. "But he's really modest about his work and very businesslike."

"I'm glad to hear it." They ate in silence after that, Thor finally shoving his chowder bowl away after pursuing a last piece of potato. "Bayne seems pretty damned interested in ol' George. I wonder what the connection is?"

Paige put her soup spoon carefully on the saucer as she finished. "I haven't a clue. Maybe the man just wanted a visit to the ocean. That's not so strange—especially since he's a fisherman, too. Mr. Bayne wants to make sure that he has a good time."

"In that case, why didn't he take him out himself?"

"Because he had other things to do, I suppose." Paige gestured as she spoke, fortunately missing her shrimp louie as the waitress stopped by their table. "Mmm—that looks almost too attractive to eat."

"Nothing fits in that category as far as I'm concerned," Thor said, passing her a roll. "And if you want to make everybody happy, eat every bit of it. Send any back and the salad chef will take it as a personal affront."

Paige smiled and picked up her fork. "I've never had a better excuse for ignoring my diet. Why on earth didn't I order chocolate torte for dessert while I was about it?"

Thor grinned in response and shook his head. "It's not the same."

"Why not?"

"The pastry chef works nights so he's already gone home."

She winced. "You really know how to hurt a person."

"Look at it from a positive side," he insisted. "You're saving your waistline."

"My waistline can look out for itself. Chocolate torte is almost medicinal."

"How do you figure that?"

"Well, therapeutic at least. I've had a hard morning." She took another bite of her salad and chewed reflectively. "Besides, there aren't any practicing psychiatrists in the Cove and I need all the help I can get these days."

"I didn't know you went in for psychiatrists," Thor said, looking surprised.

"I don't usually. But I may change my ways by the time Janet gets back from her honeymoon."

Thor grinned and seemed to relax as lunch progressed. It wasn't until they'd both finished generous pieces of torte and a second cup of coffee that Paige looked at her watch and gasped. "I didn't realize it was so late!" She directed a regretful look at the peaceful expanse of beach below the dining room windows. "As much as I hate to leave all this, I have to get back to work."

"Why?" Thor glanced at his own watch. "It isn't very late. I won't tell your boss and you don't punch a time clock. So who's to know?"

"I promised. Besides, I have a lot to get through this afternoon." She stood up and reached for her purse. "Unfortunately, I don't accomplish as much as Liza, and one of these days Alan Bayne will start asking for a cheaper day rate or a new secretary."

Thor got leisurely to his feet. "Not unless there's something drastically wrong with his eyesight. With that dress, you might even put in for a raise."

"Even after the chocolate torte?"

He stopped to let his gaze rake over her. "From this distance, I'd say it's all settled in nicely."

It was hard to leave, but Paige finally managed it ten minutes later, after Thor walked her out to the Conquistador's parking area. Since she was behind schedule, she didn't waste any time at the local bookseller's in picking up her newest armload of required reading. The clerk obviously thought that Paige was on the weird side when she made a fast sweep of the shelves, but that didn't stop him from accepting her money and giving her a complimentary shopping bag to hold the newest selections.

Getting in the car again, Paige headed straight for the house and an afternoon of concentrated work. She was turning in the driveway before she noticed a workman on the side path leading to the annex. He stopped when she braked in the carport and almost reluctantly retraced his footsteps.

Paige frowned as she got out of the car, wondering if the man had emerged from the panel truck she saw parked across the street. He was wearing denim coveralls, but there wasn't any firm name in evidence on the pocket. "Could I help you with something?" she asked crisply as he hesitated by the carport.

He pulled a slip of paper from his pocket and drawled, "Not unless you ordered a television repair."

"You must have the wrong house," she said. Her denial wasn't as strong as it should have been because she suddenly wondered if Alan had discovered something wrong with his television and called for a repairman without letting her know.

The hesitation must have been evident to the repairman. He looked at his paper again, saying, "It's this address, lady, and whoever called said it was the house at the rear. I'd better check it out."

"That depends." There wasn't any mistaking the authority in Paige's voice. "What name were you given?"

"Saunders is what I was told," the man said, sounding belligerent. "Does that mean anything to you?"

"Not a thing."

"Well, then, I'll go check it out."

"I have a better idea." Paige's words stopped him in his tracks as she gestured toward the beige car which had pulled up alongside his truck. Turning back to the repairman, she said, "That's the chief of police over there. He can help you find where the Saunderses live. We didn't call a repairman here."

She watched with satisfaction as he slowly crossed the road and exchanged a few words with the policeman. Finally, he got back in his truck and was escorted toward the highway.

The incident didn't give her reason to let her imagination run riot, Paige told herself as she collected her armload of books from the car and went in the house. There had been erring repairmen before and undoubtedly would be again—especially in a village like Cameron Cove where addresses sounded like clues from a scavenger hunt.

On impulse, she made a quick trip to the annex, returning the manuscript pages she'd typed during her stint in Janet's office. A cursory glance showed that nothing had been changed during the morning.

Before leaving, she lingered to switch on the television set and nodded in relief when the picture flashed on the screen.

Once back in her own house, she changed into comfortable jeans and settled onto the couch for more required reading. It should have been easy to concentrate; the house was quiet, with only the rustling of a few birds in the shrubbery cutting through the still air. Outside, the afternoon sun disappeared behind the cloud cover and soft, sporadic gusts of breeze rustled the rhododendron foliage against the cedar siding. Just the type of day for escapist reading, Paige knew, and was frustrated when Alan's features became superimposed on the rock-jawed heroes despite her efforts to keep him out. When it came to the love scenes, it was even worse. The fondling and caressing seemed as flat as the paper they were written on, and her interest suffered the same fate.

After skimming the second novel and almost falling asleep during a five-page-long seduction scene, she heard the ringing of the phone in outright relief. Her spirits took a nosedive a minute later, however, at Liza's words over the wire.

"I'm glad I caught you in, Paige. Something's come up and we've sort of changed our plans. I wanted to let you know so you wouldn't worry. Maybe you could tell Alan if George can't get in touch with him."

"Hold on a minute—don't hang up. What do you mean, things have changed?"

"Well, nothing was biting earlier so we didn't go

out, but now the skipper thinks we'll have a better chance."

"Slow down, will you," Paige interrupted. "What time will you be coming back tonight?"

Liza's reply was unusually breathless for such a sensible woman. "I'm not sure. I promised to cook dinner for George afterward because he hasn't had anything decent since he came to the beach."

Paige frowned as she thought about that. "Does that mean you'll be going to your house?"

"I suppose so. Of course, if we're late getting back here . . ."

"Where's here?"

"Depoe Bay," Liza said, sounding surprised. "I thought you knew."

"I guess I did, but I was half-asleep when you left this morning. All right, then I'll expect you when I see you. Is everything okay in the meantime?"

"Oh, yes!"

In any other woman, the sigh that accompanied those words would have been termed blissful. Paige's eyes widened as she heard it. "Well, I hope you have a good time," she managed finally.

"You won't forget to tell Alan if he asks about us?"

It was amazing how quickly they'd gotten on a first-name basis, Paige thought. Unbelievable, really, when most of Cameron Cove's inhabitants didn't rate that category where Liza was concerned. "I'll tell him," she promised.

"Good. Anything new with you?" Liza asked in an obvious afterthought.

"Not really," Paige had to admit. "It's getting to the point where I look forward to watching the redwoods grow."

"Too bad. Well, Alan should be back soon."

"What does that have to do with it?"

The other's laughter bubbled over the wire. "If you don't know, then you *are* in a bad way. I'll talk to you later."

Paige hung up and shoved her hands in her pockets. So much for her attempts at a nice, aloof cover. If a casual observer like Liza could see through it, she was in trouble. By the time Alan returned, she'd better work out a more successful facade.

The phone rang again as she headed for the kitchen to check the contents of the refrigerator. She snatched up the receiver, hoping her ESP was working on the right channel this time.

Unfortunately, the deep masculine tones at the other end of the wire weren't the ones she hoped to hear. "Miss Kendall? This is Chief Sherwood. Any more trouble at your place?"

The memory of his earlier appearance made her voice warm as she replied, "No, but it was a wonderful coincidence that you appeared when you did. I wasn't sure about that repair man. Between the mental patients and intruders around here, I'm a little jumpy."

He chuckled. "That's to be expected, and it wasn't a coincidence I was on hand. I promised Mr. Bayne to increase our patrols in the neighborhood for a while. Incidentally, you don't have to worry about the repairman."

"You mean he was a legitimate workman?"

"He's been around town off and on," the chief concurred. "Casual labor mostly, and there is a family at the other end of the beach named Saunders who had their television repaired recently. Apparently the date on the work order got mixed. This guy got Thor Goransen to vouch for him. Goransen told me that he's done maintenance work at the Conquistador."

"Then I was just imagining things," Paige said in relief.

"It would seem so. You might keep your eyes open, though. If any other strangers come around, give us a call. That's what you're paying taxes for."

"Thanks very much, I certainly will. And this is one case where I'm getting my money's worth. If you ever want to run for mayor, I'll send in an absentee vote."

He laughed and said, "I'll remember. And give Mr. Bayne my best."

Paige hung up, a bemused look on her face. First Liza and then a police chief. Talk about winning friends and influencing people! A pity that Alan didn't waste any of that vaunted charm with his temporary secretary and landlady. Of course—if she were being strictly honest—she hadn't exuded too much charm herself when they were together. All he had to do was walk in the door and she either dropped something, insulted him, or generally behaved like a demented creature who had more than the required number of holes in her head.

It probably came from a literary diet of lusting and frustrated characters, she told herself as she poured a glass of milk and drank it. And if she stayed in the kitchen to reconsider her plight, she'd be lusting for a wedge of banana bread to go with the milk and frustrated because she didn't need it. The only sensible thing was to go for a walk and enjoy some fresh air instead.

The dusk of late afternoon was just starting to descend by the time she made her way back from the almost-deserted beach. It had taken longer than she'd planned because she'd lingered in the Cove hunting for agates before she went across the bar to the ocean side. She'd found a handful of small stones at the water's edge and experienced as much triumph as if she'd turned up silver dollars.

An instant later, a rustling at the end of a driftwood log captured all her attention. Peering cautiously beyond the stub of a branch, she saw a tangled piece of fishing net with a large seagull help captive in its midst. "Oh, Lord!" she muttered unhappily, and went down on her knees to free it. She immediately regretted her action when the bird tried to avoid her, fluttering violently in its trap as it sensed new danger.

Paige set back on her heels trying to assess the damage. She saw that, while the gull's wings were apparently all right, one of its legs had been broken in earlier struggles to free itself.

"Take it easy, boy. Just let me think a minute,"

she said in a soothing tone, withdrawing still further as the bird watched her every movement. "Even if I had a knife to cut you free, that leg of yours would be in a bad way. Which means that I have to find something to carry you—like a cardboard box—and get you to a vet somehow." She rose to her feet. "I'll be back—just as quick as I can."

She didn't waste any more time after that, hurrying up the path through the trees to the house. By the time she finally reached her backyard, she was breathing hard and trying to ignore a painful stitch in her side. Reluctant to waste a minute, she went straight to the carport where she'd remembered seeing a carton which Janet had left half-full of Seth's clothes in readiness for the church rummage sale.

Alan found her spilling them ruthlessly out on the counter next to the rock tumbler when he came into the carport a minute or two later. "What in the dickens is going on?" he wanted to know.

Paige jumped a good three inches at his unexpected appearance. "You startled me! I didn't know you were back."

"I haven't been long. You came up that path like the devil himself was after you, so I thought I'd better check."

She shook her head impatiently as she turned back to her task. "I'm all right, but there's a seagull down on the beach that's in trouble. That's why I need this box—I want something to carry him."

"Whoa! Calm down and start over again," he said, taking the box from her as she finally emptied it.

"I tell you, there isn't time . . ."

"All right, then, you can fill me in on the way."

"You mean you're going with me?" She stared at him, her glance taking in the crisp white shirt that topped a pair of flannel slacks. "But you're not dressed for it."

"I'm not sure what 'it' is, but I'll survive," he said, gesturing her ahead of him down the path. "You'd better go first."

She'd taken only a step or two before she stopped abruptly, causing Alan, who was on her heels, to almost carom into her. "I'm sorry," she said, "I forgot to get a knife. For cutting the fishnet."

"Will a pocketknife do?" At her nod, he turned her around with his free hand and gave her a gentle shove between the shoulder blades. "Then get going. Otherwise we'll run out of daylight. Now, tell me what kind of a rescue operation this is—"

It wasn't difficult for her to provide the details on the way back to the beach, nor did Alan waste any time sizing up the situation in the fading light once they reached the driftwood log and the hapless gull.

"I think it's better to keep him in that netting while we put him in the box," Alan said, getting down on one knee.

"You don't have to do it; you'll ruin those trousers," Paige said, trying to help and finding herself blocked by his shoulders. "What's the matter?" The last came anxiously after he swore violently on the first attempt at a transfer.

"There's nothing wrong with his beak," Alan announced, shaking his bruised hand and then trying again. "Your idea of a box is sure the right one. Here we go—*allez-oop*. Made it that time," he said, getting to his feet.

"Yes, but your hand—it's bleeding!"

"Nothing to fuss about. I'll live." He was searching his back pocket. "Where the deuce's that handkerchief?"

"In your other pocket." Before he could object, Paige pulled out the clean white square and handed it to him, watching him wrap it around his palm.

"That's got it." He hoisted the open box carefully, but stood undecided. "I'm not sure whether he'll be better off with the lid open or closed. How far is it to the vet's?"

"About two miles." She looked up at him, her face worried. "What if he's not there? It's after office hours."

"We'll call him from the house and tell him it's an emergency." He jerked his chin toward the box. "This poor guy won't last much longer in this state."

"I know." She hurried ahead of him up the path, saying over her shoulder, "I'm glad you feel that way, too."

"What did you epxect me to do, for pete's sake?"

She managed a fleeting grin as he pulled alongside on a wider part of the path. "I don't know. I haven't hit anything like this in that required reading."

"I'm not surprised. An armful of injured seagull would even slow down Casanova."

There wasn't any answer for that, and Paige contented herself with pulling back overhanging branches in the path to ease their way until they reached the house once again. Alan turned toward the carport, saying, "You go call the vet and tell him the situation. I'll see if I can cut away some of this net and make our patient more comfortable before we put him in the car."

"I'll hurry," Paige promised.

She was out again in less than five minutes, pulling a cardigan on as she came. "We're in luck. The vet's home is right next door to the office and he'll be watching for us." She paused suddenly, remembering, "What about your hand? Shouldn't you get a bandage?"

"It's fine." He jerked his head toward the wounded bird. "Jonah here is at the top of the priority list."

They installed the box with their patient on the back seat of Alan's car and set out, Paige acting as navigator when they reached the main highway. "I forgot to ask how your trip to Portland came out," she said after they'd merged with the steady steam of traffic, and then drew in her breath sharply.

Alan's foot came quickly off the accelerator. "What's wrong?"

She gestured an apology. "Sorry, I didn't mean to startle you. I'd just realized that I hadn't told you Liza called and left a message. She and George will be delayed."

"Oh." Alan's eyebrows rose but there was nothing but polite acknowledgment in his tone.

"Is that all you have to say?" Paige asked.

"What else is there?" He shot her another lightning glance. "They were getting along all right, weren't they?"

"More than all right, I gathered," she told him drily.

"Well, then. What's to worry?"

"You weren't that casual about keeping tabs on George before," she pointed out.

"That was before I met friend Liza. She should be a match for anybody. Is that the animal hospital we're looking for? Beyond that blue neon motel sign?"

"That's the one," she said, feeling a surge of relief. She turned to look into the back and check on the bird. "He seems awfully quiet. I'm not so sure he can live up to that name you gave him."

"He'll make it," Alan said confidently, as he slowed the car and turned off into the gravel parking lot of the animal hospital, pulling up in front of a brightly-lighted building. "Jonah might not be giving any thanks for his deliverance now, but wait until the vet does his job." Turning off the ignition key, he got out and reached carefully in for the box. "Come on, boy—you're about to get swallowed up by medical science. Once they splint that leg and fill you full of antibiotics, you'll be spit out into the world again fighting fit."

Paige came around to close the door once he had the box in his arms. "Now I'm beginning to believe you *are* a writer," she said, following him up the path. "Before this, you'd sounded more like a systems analyst or a—" She broke off as a dark-haired young man in a white coat met them on the threshold. "Dr. Harlan? I'm Paige Kendall and this is Alan Bayne."

"Complete with feathered friend," Alan said.

"I'm all ready for you," the doctor said amiably. "Just bring the box on through to the surgery, Mr. Bayne, and we'll see what can be done."

"If you don't need me, I'll wait here," Paige said, subsiding in a chair by the door. She found it hard to focus on the news magazine she'd picked up from a nearby table until several minutes passed and it became apparent that Jonah was going to have a future after all. Then she relaxed and concentrated on the magazine's contents, leafing casually through the pages, until a picture and article in the science section made her stiffen on her chair.

Both men found her staring down at it when they came out of the surgery ten minutes later. "I'll put a splint on that leg while he's under the anesthetic," the doctor was telling Alan. "By tomorrow morning, he should be eating again and on the road back. Of course, it'll take a while for the leg to heal, but I don't anticipate any problems."

"Do you want to keep him here or could he be kept in a cage at home?" Alan asked. "If my landlady doesn't mind another tenant," he went on, smiling at Paige.

"No, of course not." She brought her thoughts back to Jonah with an effort. "Then he's going to be all right?"

"Thanks to the two of you. I doubt if he would have lasted through the night in that fishing net,"

Dr. Harlan said. "Check with me in the morning and I'll have more of a prognosis then."

"Thanks very much—we'll do that," Alan said, opening the door for Paige. As he led the way back to the car, he said, "Now, maybe we can have dinner. We can eat with a clear conscience, too. Jonah's in good hands and seemed to know it. I like your vet—no beating around the bush."

"Everything out in the open, huh?" Paige commented drily once they'd gotten in the car again. "Well, that makes a change, at least."

Alan had started the engine and was pulling back out onto the highway when her meaning penetrated. Instead of accelerating, he let the motor idle, the car still on the shoulder of the road. "I hoped we could bury the hatchet, but not between my shoulder blades. What are you talking about?"

She shrugged elaborately. "You wanted me to do research."

He surveyed her carefully in the dim dashboard light. "Don't tell me that the newest batch of required reading has gotten to you. I didn't expect you to take it seriously."

"I'll remember that," she told him levelly, "but the reading isn't what's bothering me. I want to know why you've been so quiet about mentioning that old George is really Dr. George Porter—one of this country's leading scientists in synthetic fuels."

After a considerable pause, Alan muttered something that Paige sensibly ignored. "I suppose you'd like an explanation," he said finally, before turning onto the highway.

"Any time." There was triumph in her manner as she checked the watch on her wrist. "Preferably in the next ten minutes. That is, if you still want a roof over your head tonight and a secretary in the morning."

Chapter Six

"I don't like threats," Alan replied, sounding all the more ominous because of the soft, deliberate spacing of his words.

"And I don't like people who hide behind half-truths," she said, staying determinedly with her principles. "Maybe at the beginning you had an excuse, but after the break-in you could have told me. And don't bring in that escaped mental patient routine as a red herring." When he simply shrugged and accelerated without replying, she went on a little less doggedly, "You didn't really think that was who stuffed me in the closet, did you?"

"At this point, I'd have trouble spelling my last name, so don't ask me any sixty-four dollar questions. Frankly, I'd feel better after some food. Would you prefer eating by yourself or are you willing to share a tray at the local drive-in?"

"One doesn't necessarily preclude the other," she

told him, unwilling to find herself on the defensive so soon.

He muttered something unintelligible—or perhaps he was just grinding his teeth. Paige hoped it was the latter and waited to find out. "All right, you win," he said finally. "I'm not partial to camping out on the beach at this time of year, and I still need some typing done."

"So you'll explain?" she asked, trying to hide her triumph.

"I'll tell you all you need to know."

"I don't know when I've heard a more charming apology," she told him sweetly, and added, "there's a good drive-in down there on the left," before he could snap back at her.

After that, their only outward disagreement was whether they needed two orders of french fries to go with the hamburgers or whether one large one would do. They settled for the latter, and onion rings on the side.

"What I can't see is why you had to be so hush-hush about what George did," Paige said, leaning back in her corner of the front seat and nursing a mug of coffee while they waited for the rest of their order. "You made him sound like some erratic character who enjoyed going steady with a vodka bottle on his vacation." When a crooked grin softened Alan's expression, she frowned in disbelief. "You mean I'm right?"

"Well, George has had his moments in the past." Alan took a swallow of his own coffee and swirled the remaining liquid absently. "It's not surprising, though. The last six months have meant nothing but pressure for him. I don't know exactly what that magazine article said about him . . ."

"It was about the success of his experiments for synthetic fuel," she said, trying to remember exactly. "Whatever that means."

"Just what it says. George has come up with a real winner, we think. Basically, it involves converting coal to fuel oil."

Her forehead wrinkled as she assessed his words. "That takes lots of money to develop, doesn't it?"

"You bet your Aunt Nelly—you wouldn't believe how much! That's why the company's in the running for a government subsidy."

She chewed on her bottom lip, still puzzled. "But what does all this have to do with you? Unless you're using George's background for a character study—" She broke off abruptly as his shoulders moved with laughter. "Oh, Lord, now what have I said?"

He shook his head, getting his amusement under control. "If George suspected anything like that, he'd take off for our nearest competitor and probably sue for character defamation as well. I wouldn't blame him." When she still stared wordlessly, he explained, "I'm one of the major stockholders in the company that employs George. Writing is just a hobby of mine; the rest of the time I'm an engineer." His expression became wry. "This is the first time I've come close to combining the two jobs, and look what the hell has happened!"

"I'm not sure, but I think I've just been insulted—any way you look at it."

"I didn't mean it was all your fault," he added hastily.

"Thanks very much. I can understand why you went in for engineering rather than diplomacy. With your tact, you'd stir up a global war without even trying."

He grinned, clearly unabashed, and watched while their carhop brought the food. Handing over a hamburger after she'd gone again, he said, "I did plan to take you out for a decent dinner, but that was another idea of mine that went off the tracks."

"You didn't know that you were going to run an ambulance service for Jonah. Besides, I like hamburgers, and if you'll move that order of onion rings where I can reach it, all is forgiven."

His grin broadened as he complied and watched her take a satisfied bite. "At least I'll know how to improve your disposition if you threaten to throw me out in the cold again."

"Well, unless you come through with some salient facts, you'll need to furnish a steady diet of hamburgers. Was this strictly a holiday jaunt for George?" As he hesitated, she fixed him with a severe look. "The truth, please. Yes or no."

"There isn't a one-word answer," he protested. "George needed a rest; he was approaching the ragged edge after all his research and that wasn't good. Fishing is better therapy than a psychiatrist or sitting around an apartment."

Paige selected another onion ring with care. "That's all very well, but I feel you're still leaving out some of the essentials."

"Like what?"

"Like who stuffed me in the closet and what were they looking for in the annex? And *don't* tell me it was the neighborhood fiend."

His lips twitched. "I wasn't about to. Although there's still an escaped patient, so it's a good idea to lock the doors."

"You don't have to remind me. I was thinking about that when the repairman appeared on the path this afternoon." As Alan's head jerked up, she waved the remnant of hamburger airily. "Simmer down. It was a false alarm. Chief Sherwood cruised by and checked him out. Apparently the man has done casual labor around the Cove and he just had the wrong address. Thor vouched for him when the police called."

"I see." Alan took the last bite of his own hamburger and put the foil wrapping back on the tray at his elbow. "How about some dessert?"

"No, thanks." She started handing the few leftovers to him, brushing some remaining crumbs from the front seat. "Incidentally, I finished that typing you gave me so you can check it when we get home."

"Let's leave it until tomorrow." He sounded preoccupied as he turned on his headlights to summon the carhop. "Actually, there are a couple of things I still have to do tonight. When did Liza say George would be back?"

"She didn't. We could drive past her house and check if anybody's home."

A smile lightened his face momentarily. "I don't think that would win a popularity contest."

"I didn't mean to peer through the curtains, for heaven's sake."

"I'm glad that reading all those books has taught you something," he said austerely.

"You make me sound like a prying—" She stopped abruptly, noting the amusement on his face. "Unless I'm wrong, I just rose to the bait again." She leaned back to survey him more carefully. "Exactly how many research projects do you have going?"

"I'm still a little hazy on the development of my female characters. That's where I hope you can provide the help."

She stared, not quite sure whether he was serious. "I've almost exhausted the sexy novels in the book stores here."

"Don't worry about it." He squinted to see his watch in the dim light. "Damn! It's later than I thought. Don't bother with any more reading or typing tonight. We can go over the stuff tomorrow when I'm around."

"You mean you're going away again? But you just got back." Too late, she heard the wail of protest in her voice and tried to sound matter-of-fact as she went on, "I thought you meant there were things to do around the house."

"There's no need for you to be nervous; I'll check out your place before I leave. And don't argue about it," he added when she started to protest. "That's one thing I have learned about women. They feel a compulsion to have the last word."

"Like now?" she asked, and smiled at his exasperated groan.

It didn't take long for them to drive back to the darkened, deserted house, and despite the objections Paige also felt compelled to voice, she was happy to have his tall figure stalking ahead of her once she unlocked the front door.

She watched Alan make a quick but thorough survey of the empty rooms, and when he came back into the front hall again, she asked, "What do I tell Liza if she calls again? Or George?"

"You might find out if they caught anything worth eating."

"Be serious, won't you?"

"I am. I doubt if they'll be calling for any advice." He lingered by the door with his hand on the knob. "Since you're an expert in the field of affection these days, did it occur to you that Liza and George might be a nicely matched pair?"

"But Liza doesn't trust men. At least that's what she's always said."

"Until now?" Alan was watching her expressive face with interest.

"You might be right. When she called earlier—she giggled." Paige's solemn pronouncement was tantamount to the walls of Jericho starting to crumble.

Alan grinned. "Absolutely the beginning of the end. To think I could have saved all of that money you've spent on passion and pulchritude. Well, that's the way it goes. Lock your door and don't worry about the fiend; he'll have a hard time getting past that patrol car parked at the end of the road."

Paige could have told him that none of the lusting heroes in paperbacks ever left a woman with an absentminded pat on the derriere, especially if they expected any cooperation in the next chapter. Unfortunately, by then Alan had pulled the door closed behind him and checked to make sure that the lock held, before his footsteps disappeared off the porch.

She didn't sleep very well once she got to bed. It was ridiculous to miss Alan's presence in the guest room across the hall, especially since she'd prided herself on living alone and liking it for the past year or so. Life made no sense at all, she told herself crossly, and thumped her pillow again, trying to find a comfortable niche.

Under ordinary circumstances when she couldn't get to sleep, she simply picked up a book and read until they lived happily ever after or the print blurred—whichever came first. But two afternoons of enforced reading made her reluctant to approach another printed page unless it was a crossword puzzle.

That was a flop, too, and she finally took her pillow out to the living room and watched a swing shift horror movie on television. Fortunately, she fell soundly asleep before the heroine was abducted by a bat-winged monster, and didn't stir until the phone rang the next morning.

She found herself tangled in the afghan she'd put over her feet and stared, puzzled, at the television test pattern until she remembered the night before.

The phone was on its fifth ring when she finally

reached the receiver, and Thor sounded aggrieved when he heard her voice.

"I was just about to hang up," he complained. "What took you so long?"

"It's still the middle of the night," she protested before checking the kitchen clock. "At least it's only seven-thirty."

"Most of us working people," he said, emphasizing the last two words, "can't afford to loll around in bed. I certainly expected you to be up by now."

"I am," she said, trying to keep her annoyance in check. "But I'm not promising anything when I hang up. Besides, you must have me mixed up with somebody else. I didn't leave a wake-up call with your switchboard."

"Very funny." His tone belied his words, and there wasn't anything remotely humorous about his next statement. "I thought you might be concerned about your pal George."

"What do you mean? What's happened?"

"Your guess is as good as mine. The only sure thing is that he didn't come back to the hotel last night. The floor maid reported this morning that his bed hadn't been slept in."

Until his last sentence, Paige hadn't been aware that she was holding her breath. She let it out in relief as she said, "Is *that* all? Surely it's happened before at the Conquistador."

"That's not the point. And I'm not worried about collecting his bill," Thor went on virtuously. "People have been known to get in trouble on fishing expeditions around here. There was a chance you'd want to check with the Coast Guard."

"At Depoe Bay?" Paige brushed her hair back from her cheeks and tried to think rationally. "But why? They'd get in touch with Chief Sherwood if there were trouble. Everybody knows that Liza comes from Cameron Cove." She stretched the coiled phone cord as she moved over and pushed aside the kitchen curtain, peering out the window. "Besides, the weather doesn't look too bad—a little gray but that's nothing new."

"That's for now. There were storm warnings during the night. A fishing boat got caught crossing the bar further north and they had an experienced crew aboard."

"I'm sorry to hear it, but I still don't think there's any need to worry about George and Liza. When she phoned, she said they might be delayed."

"Why?" Thor cut in tersely.

"Something about the tides, I think." Paige rubbed her forehead, trying to remember. "It might not hurt to check with Alan."

"Go ahead—I'll wait."

Paige drew in her breath. "Sorry to disappoint you—but you'll have to hang up so I can phone him at the annex. Why don't you call back later?"

She hung up in the middle of his, "Paige, I'm sorry . . ." and started for the bathroom to shower so she wouldn't hear the phone in case he called right back.

Even after she'd showered and dressed, she was reluctant to call Alan regarding George's whereabouts.

She was virtually certain that there was no reason for alarm and that Thor's phone call was ninety-nine percent curiosity with one percent true concern.

She was still wondering what to do about it as she went out to the carport to change the grit in Seth's tumbler. The agates would be worn away by the time Alan could fit the changeover into his schedule, she told herself. Unfortunately, he caught her hosing down the gleaming rocks a little later when he came up the back path. "I thought there was something interesting going on," he said, eyeing the stones keenly. "Why didn't you let me know?"

"Just for a glance at my nephew's agates?" she asked wryly, holding a small specimen up to the light. "They probably have a market value of a half dollar, *after* they're polished."

"What does that have to do with it?" he asked, taking the hose from her hand and washing the last remnants of milky grit from the walk. "How long have they been tumbling?"

"Seth told me it's the third week. Now they're ready for the last go-round. They should come out of this in mint condition." She held up an amber beauty and pursed her lips as she considered it. "Maybe I was wrong about the market value."

Alan grinned. "Sure you were. They'd sell for a dollar at least. Besides, the net worth isn't important —it's the spirit of the chase. Can anybody find agates around here?"

She nodded and looked at him challengingly. "For a fee, I could be tempted to take you to one of the good beds."

He seemed amused. "Expert guide service?"

"And then some. Liza may know about fishing, but Seth and I have the corner on agate hunting. Oh!" Her palm flew up to her mouth. "I was supposed to ask you about Liza and George. Thor called a while ago. Apparently, lots of people slept at the Conquistador last night, but George wasn't one of them."

Alan kept his attention on the tumbler of agates, stirring the wet stones with his finger. "It can't be the first time that's happened."

"You're a cynic," Paige told him, glancing up from measuring tablespoons of polishing powder into the drum for the final tumbling period. "So am I, I guess, because I said practically the same thing."

"It didn't occur to him that Liza and George might be safe but otherwise occupied?"

Paige leveled the last tablespoon of powder carefully. "Of course, but people always suspect the worst. I don't think Liza is the type for sleeping around. And it's important to preserve her reputation in a small town."

"I don't quibble with that. Here, let me fasten that for you." He took the tumbler from her after she'd added a modicum of water and secured the top. Then he put the drum back on the cradle and plugged in the cord. The low, grinding noise sounded again as the tumbler went around steadily on its base.

"Same time next week," Paige announced, rinsing the remaining grit from her fingers and drying them on a towel that Janet had left weighted with a rawhide bone, to show that it was reserved for dog baths.

Alan hefted the bone experimentally. "Where's the dog that belongs to this?" he wanted to know.

"Turk? He's staying with one of my nephew's chums down the street." Paige smiled as she put the towel back on the counter. "It's just as well. The front porch of the annex is his favorite place for naps, and there's not much room to spare when a sheepdog is in residence."

Alan grinned in response, shoving his hands in his jeans pockets. "An old English one, eh? That's the breed you pet in the middle until you find out which end wags."

"You've got it. But how did we get off George and Liza onto this subject?"

"Forget them—they're okay. As a matter of fact, George checked in with me last night."

Paige started to say, "Why didn't you mention it?" until she realized that there was no reason he should have gone shouting it about the neighborhood. "I'll tell Thor that he can stop worrying," she murmured finally.

"The weather's not bad," Alan said, looking overhead as they walked toward her back porch. "How about having breakfast on the beach while you show me how to hunt agates?"

She appeared to consider it, finally saying, "All right," when she decided that she'd shown proper reluctance. Then she spoiled the effect by adding, "I'm practically ready to go, once I get a jacket.

Unless you're talking about a formal picnic with a beach fire and eggs and bacon."

"Lord, no. I've fixed a flask of coffee and put some sweet rolls in a rucksack. Will that do?"

"It sounds great! Let me contribute a couple of cans of juice from the refrigerator."

"Fair enough. I'll get my jacket and meet you back here in . . ." He paused suggestively.

"Five minutes. It's a minus tide this morning so that means good hunting. And put some boots on because we'll be in the wet sand."

His sudden grin took years from his face. "Yes, ma'am."

"Are you sure you've never gone looking for agates before?" she asked, suspicious of his lurking amusement.

"I've never gone agate hunting here before," he said, raising his hand solemnly. "And you'll have to give me an extra two minutes so I can find some socks to go in the boots."

He was gone before she could reply. Perhaps it was just as well, she thought. There was no point in reminding him that she'd noted his evasive reply about rock hunting. All it really took was an infinite amount of patience and the proper locale to collect agates. She could supply the latter and it would be interesting to see if Alan could summon enough of the former to rank as a true rockhound.

The ringing of the phone interrupted her while she was putting the juice cans in a plastic bag. She closed the refrigerator door and snatched up the receiver, hoping that Janet might be calling from the islands. "Hello?"

"I thought you were going to call me back," Thor said, not bothering to beat about the bush.

"Oh, it's you." She realized too late that she hadn't bothered with diplomacy, either. "I'm sorry, it's just that I thought Janet might be calling."

"She wouldn't be phoning now. With the time difference, it's still the middle of the night there."

"Well, she could have had insomnia," Paige retorted, trying for the defensive and losing again when he started to laugh.

"On a honeymoon?" he said when he could control his voice. "For God's sake, Paige—use your head."

"Okay—so I'm an idiot," she agreed, frowning as she checked her watch. "We can discuss that another time. Right now I have a date with an agate bed."

"First things first. Did you find out anything about George?"

She nodded and then realized the futility of such a gesture. "He's okay. I would have called you later."

"You mean you've heard from him?" Thor asked, ignoring her last remark.

"Well, I didn't, but Alan did. Last night. Everything was fine."

"Don't tell me George is still with your man-hating secretary."

"I won't tell you because I haven't the foggiest notion. And I don't know why you pick on Liza. What did she ever do to you?"

"You'd never get to the agate beds if I started telling you," he retorted cynically. "Come on and have breakfast with me later if you really want to know. How about it?"

"Actually, I have a breakfast date. Alan wants to try his luck as a rockhound—"

"So it's Alan now. What happened to Mr. Bayne?"

"We sort of buried the hatchet."

"And obviously not in the right place. I thought you had better taste. Don't worry, I'll still be around to help you pick up the pieces afterward."

"You've made my day," she retorted with the frankness of lengthy acquaintance. Just then, she saw Alan's tall form come up to the back door and she said hastily, "Thor, I must go."

"Okay." There was a pause and then he said, "I'm sorry I lost my temper, love."

"Forget it. We'll talk another time," she told him, and hung up before he could delay her any longer. Hurrying to the back door, she flung it open, saying, "Sorry, I got caught on the phone. The juice is on the counter. Give me a minute to get a jacket and I'll be with you."

"Take your time," Alan called after her as she started down the hallway. "The agates won't run away. Incidentally, you weren't the only one with a phone call. Dr. Harlan just got in touch with me."

Paige froze with one arm still out of her jacket sleeve. "Jonah! Is he all right?"

"Better than the doc dared hope. He says he'll be as good as new when the leg mends."

"That's wonderful!" She shrugged into her jacket and turned a thoughtful face when she'd finished with the zipper. "Did he say anything about moving

Jonah here to recover? He doesn't have to stay at the hospital, does he?"

"I shouldn't think so. We can find out when we visit him," Alan replied, slinging the small nylon rucksack on his shoulder.

Paige stood back to inspect him. "I thought you'd have a burlap bag with you, too."

"To carry the agates?" He grinned and patted the front of his own quilted jacket. "Don't let appearances deceive you. The pockets in this thing are deep enough to hide a basketball player. Are you ready? Let's go."

It was amazing how quickly they covered the path to the beach. Paige found herself half-running to keep up until Alan obligingly shortened his steps.

"Why didn't you holler 'yoicks' or something?" he asked, watching her catch her breath.

"It wasn't important." She fell into step beside him, saying happily, "Doesn't the air smell wonderful here at the beach?"

"Just the same as damp weather anywhere," he teased, clearly enjoying her enthusiasm. "And I forgot to bring my umbrella."

"I haven't seen you with an . . ." Her voice trailed off as she remembered her fateful description of him that first morning. She'd bequeathed him a pair of rubbers, too, and from the look on his face he wasn't about to ignore it. "Don't you ever forget anything?" she asked despairingly.

"Not if I can use it for legitimate blackmail," he retorted, holding back an overhanging cedar branch still soggy with dew. By then, they were almost at the bottom of the trail, which spilled onto the wide sandy beach some fifty feet beyond. There was a spiny ridge on the narrow neck of land, curving to the right to form the arm of the cove that gave the hamlet its name. A handful of expensive summer homes were atop the ridge but not many, because an unusually high tide or midwinter storm accompanied by gale force winds sent the surf surging over the bulkheads. Only a few diehard residents with bulging bank accounts were willing to take the risks for the view. The net result was a stretch of land inhabited mainly by gulls and beach lovers who didn't disclose the location of their favorite haunt to strangers.

When Paige and Alan arrived at the edge of the surf, only one other person could be seen far up the shore, throwing sticks for a black dog.

"What's first on the agenda?" Alan wanted to know. "Food or hunting for treasure?"

She broke out laughing. "If you're talking about agates, they'll end up *costing* you money."

"Who cares about that? What do you say to searching for a half-hour and then stopping for breakfast?"

"Fair enough."

"Hey! Where are you going?" he called after her when she started up across the ridge toward the rocky slope of the cove on the other side.

She grinned mischievously back at him. "That would be telling. You're on your own now, but whoever gets the most agates has his breakfast served in style."

He saluted her, laughing, and dropped his ruck-sack at the end of a driftwood stump before strolling down to the damp sand on the ocean side to start his search.

It was about twenty minutes later before Paige heard his boots behind her and straightened to greet him. "Any luck?"

"Not too many, but I settled for quality instead of quantity." He held up an orange specimen the size of a brazil nut and allowed her to admire it. "I have a couple more in my pocket—not as big, but not bad," he said smugly. "How about you?"

"I'm a great believer in quantity," she said, and brought out a fistful of small stones in varying colors.

He whistled, impressed, and then reached for a red, egg-shaped one. "That's not agate."

"I know. It's jasper, but it looks beautiful when it's polished. I wasn't going to include it in my to-tal."

He shook his head in surrender as he watched her pocket her hoard carefully. "I know when I'm beaten. Come on, I'll feed you, and then watch out! If it's quantity that counts, this is the place to look." He bent and triumphantly filched a gleaming white agate just inches from the toe of her boot. Solemnly tucking it away, he then reached for her hand, and grimaced when he felt how cold it was. "Let's go. You need that coffee even more than I do."

Paige had forgotten how much fun spur-of-the-moment beach picnics could be. They settled in the shelter of the driftwood log to avoid the occasional bursts of wind which swept the long expanse of beach, and resolutely ignored the invasion of sand. Fortunately, the juice cans were impervious to grit and they stashed the thermos cups of coffee carefully on an outcropping driftwood branch, so it was only the sweet rolls that had to be watched with care. Even then, they had triumphed until Alan attempted to pour more coffee and brushed his sandy sleeve over the remaining Danish. "Oh, hell!" he said vehemently, seeing what he'd done.

"It's all right. Maybe I can dust off the top— there's just a little bit of sand." Paige reached in her jacket pocket for a handkerchief to brush the grit from her fingers and wrinkled her nose comically to find she'd stored her agates in the same pocket. "Do *you* have a clean handkerchief?" she asked Alan, sprawled out beside her.

"Sure." His hand moved and then stopped midway. "It's in my hip pocket," he said with some disgust. "Wouldn't you know!"

Since they were both scrunched against the log to avoid the wind, his hip pockets undoubtedly had more than their quota of sand.

"It doesn't matter. I've had enough to eat," Paige told him diplomatically.

"You're a terrible liar." He sighed as he wrapped the sandy pastry in a piece of plastic and put it back in the rucksack. Brushing his hands off, he picked up his coffee cup and arranged himself comfortably back against the log beside her. "I'm learning things all the time. No wonder people make love on a beach.

It's the same theory as a power failure in crowded cities."

Paige's pulse reacted to his comment like a shore bird fluttering to avoid an oncoming wave. "All right, I'll play straight man," she said in a wary tone. "What's the connection between a beach picnic and a power failure at home?"

He gestured with his free hand to emphasize his point. "In both instances, you have too much spare time and practically no way to utilize it."

Paige replaced her empty coffee cup in the rucksack, keeping her gaze carefully lowered. "I'm overcome with such splendid logic. There must be some kind of moral still to come."

"Well, take now, for instance—we can't spend any more time eating in these surroundings, but it's comfortable for other things."

"The same things that happen during power failures all over the world?"

"Exactly."

"I don't see why you needed me to do any research," she told him. "You've worked this out pretty well on your own."

"Strictly theory," he responded solemnly. "It would help to put it to the test."

"That's ridiculous! If you think I'm going to lie here and—"

"Conduct social experiments?" he filled in, his lips twitching. "Hardly. Besides, you're not the type, so relax."

Reassured by his calm, matter-of-fact response, she did just that, stretching out again beside his tall figure and surveying him covertly as he studied a flock of tiny seabirds nearby. She watched the pulse beating steadily just below his stern jaw line and let her gaze wander to his dark hair, tousled slightly by the wind. He'd half-closed his eyes against the glare of the surf, allowing her to notice for the first time how thick his lashes were and imagine how annoyed he'd be if she mentioned it. Her glance proceeded leisurely down to his bulky jacket pockets where he'd carefully stored his hoard of agates. Her lips curved as she recalled that event; anyone would have thought he'd been picking up pieces of eight from the way he'd displayed his finds! It was a strange reaction from a man who wore an outward air of sophistication as easily as his nylon jacket. Her eyes went back to note how broad his shoulders looked under that jacket while, at the same time, his worn jeans showed there wasn't any extra flesh at his hips or thighs.

Suddenly she realized her recent reading must have made more of an impression than she'd thought. Never before had she conducted such a personal inventory of a man. Thighs were something found only in the poultry section of the supermarket, she told herself sternly, and she'd better remember it!

She sighed unconsciously and then felt warmth in her cheeks as Alan's gaze focused on her again. Fortunately, all he said was, "You okay?"

"Fine. Great. Just great!" she said brightly, sounding like a freshman cheerleader with pom-poms.

What was it about the man that made her do everything wrong, she thought unhappily as his attention turned back toward the surf. He only had to enter a room for her nerve ends to start prickling. Now, when he was so close that she could feel the warmth of his body all along the length of hers, her awareness was so intense that it was a miracle he didn't feel it.

The silence between them lengthened, but Paige was unable to make herself relax. She deliberately kept her breathing shallow and measured, trying to concentrate on something—anything—rather than the man beside her. The rustle of quilted nylon as his jacket sleeve brushed hers sounded crisply in her ears, almost as loud as the cry of the lone gull soaring everhead or the clang of a halyard on the metal flagpole in front of a shuttered house down the ridge.

She risked another quick glance at Alan's profile, thankful that he was watching the gull who had swooped to land near a piece of seaweed. Alan's pulse was still beating with measured regularity in his throat. Obviously he wasn't suffering from any nervous reaction—which showed her refusal to indulge in light lovemaking hadn't bothered him. As he'd announced so calmly, she wasn't the type.

Paige frowned as she thought about it. Talk about an inflated male ego! She could certainly put his outmoded theories to the test just as well as any other woman. After all, she'd picked up a few tactics over the years without any help. Alan might as well learn that ninety-nine percent of American women didn't need steamy book passages—they could make up their own dialogue in a romantic situation.

She dwelt on that enticing prospect a minute longer and then wrapped her arms over her breast and managed to shiver delicately.

Her movement brought Alan's attention quickly back from the shore, and he frowned as he said, "That wind's gotten stronger in the last few minutes. How about some more coffee?"

"No, thanks." She looked across at him hopefully. "Maybe if you wouldn't mind serving as a wind-break . . ."

He stared back, seemingly intrigued by a close-up vision of her deep blue eyes, which, for the first time, weren't sending out a shower of sparks. When he spoke, his voice was almost gruff. "We might do better if we tried bundling."

"I think you're right, but there aren't any blankets," she pointed out, as an afterthought.

"At least I can put my arm around you and make you comfortable." His arm moved from around her shoulder to her waist, hauling her snug against him. Then he bent his head, letting his lips slide softly down her cheek, coming to rest finally at the corner of her mouth while his free hand opened the zipper of her jacket. "You're right about one thing," he said, his mouth still at the corner of her lips. "This beach life leaves a lot to be desired."

"Why is that?" she asked breathlessly, as his hand parted her jacket and wended its way to her blouse.

"There are too damned many clothes for one thing—it feels like you have a second skin."

She drew in her breath sharply as his exploration led him to the silky skin he was seeking, and then rational thinking deserted her entirely under his expert caresses.

"Is that better?" he murmured later, his lips drawing gentle diagrams on the soft skin behind her ear.

She wondered why he bothered to ask such a silly question when she was curved tightly against him, obviously enjoying every moment. "I feel marvelous. . . ."

"Warm enough now?"

"Mmm." Fortunately, he wasn't in a position to see the color that flooded her cheeks after her ecstatic murmur.

His mouth slid toward hers as he asked unevenly, "Then why didn't we do this before? I was all for it from the beginning."

"In my research, the men didn't talk so much," Paige said, closing her eyes and waiting for his lips to cover hers again.

As if from afar, she heard his heavy breathing and marveled that his sophistication wasn't any deeper than her own. Just then, Alan sounded so aroused that he was almost panting.

But even Paige's bemused euphoria couldn't let her ignore the hefty shower of sand which landed on her face at that moment. "What the dickens!" she yelped, and struggled to sit upright, stopping open-mouthed as she saw a black Labrador panting happily on the driftwood log above them. Her amazement turned to annoyance as the dog leaped down beside Alan and started licking his ear.

"My Lord, Rufus!" Alan said, pushing with difficulty up on an elbow, his other arm still around Paige.

"A friend of yours?" she asked, and then frowned as Alan looked around the tangled roots of the driftwood toward the beach. "What's going on? Do you see someone?"

He ducked to fend off another canine caress and said to her, "Just follow my lead and take that guilty look off your face! Otherwise, you'll give the whole thing away."

Before Paige could protest, Rufus' wagging tail sent another shower of sand her way, making her close her eyes hastily.

They opened again when she heard a feminine voice trill, "Oh, there you are, Rufus! Come here, you silly creature!" Rufus was dragged unwilling a few steps away, and the newcomer, a luscious brunette, said, "Alan! I had no idea!" Her voice trailed off as she noticed Paige. "I'm so sorry. I'd have kept Rufus on a leash if I'd known there was anyone about."

"No problem," Alan told her, sounding as unconcerned as if he'd been conducting a board meeting rather than huddling behind some driftwood with a blonde. "Actually, we were trying to be inconspicuous. Bird-watching doesn't work otherwise. By the way, Barb, I don't believe you've met Paige Kendall. Paige, this is Barbara Barrett."

"How do you do." The brunette, like Rufus, didn't waste much time with women, turning immediately back to Alan. "Did you say bird-watching?

You didn't mention it was a hobby of yours when we were talking last night."

"Probably because we had so many other things to discuss." Alan shoved himself to a sitting position against the log and patted Rufus on the head before directing a brief glance toward Paige. "Miss Barrett's with a real estate firm in Portland, but she concentrates on their beach property."

Paige's smile felt as if it had been pasted on. "That must mean long hours, Miss Barrett." Like last night, she wanted to add. Or did it count as work when the client was Alan Bayne? From the way he was beaming fatuously at the brunette, it was clear that he didn't. And he was so convincing that the silly woman even believed his story about bird-watching. Paige could see her wide-eyed look as he reported solemnly, "The Oregon beaches are a haven for bird life. I'm surprised that you didn't know it."

"Well, we've always stressed the scenery and the fishing and the beachcombing," Barbara Barrett responded, ticking them off on graceful fingers while Rufus collapsed nearby and started licking a paw. "This is something new to me. Is it a hobby of yours, too, Miss Kendall?"

"I'm just a newcomer to the sport." Paige got to her feet and brushed the sand off her jeans. And then, deciding that Alan might as well suffer a little, too, said, "What kind of a bird were we looking for?"

"A lammergeyer," he said indulgently, "Your memory's going."

She glared at him before turning to the other woman. "Of course—a lammergeyer—an endangered species. You'd think I could remember. Are you a bird lover, too?"

"I have trouble after robins and seagulls," the real estate woman replied, clearly bored by the topic. She turned back to Alan, whose shoulders were shaking with laughter. "What's so funny?"

"Ah—Rufus," he said promptly. "He was after a flea."

"Oh, Lord, that's why I usually keep him down on wet sand," she said, bending to snap a leash on the dog's collar. "We'll have to go. It was nice meeting you, Miss Kendall. Good luck with your bird-watching. And Alan, be sure to call me—if I can help in any way. You know where to reach me, practically anytime." She flashed him a brilliant smile and strode off, Rufus bouncing happily at her side.

Paige didn't waste any time starting back toward the path in the opposite direction.

"Hey, wait a minute!" Alan caught up with her before she'd taken more than a half-dozen steps and pulled her to a halt. "Where do you think you're going?"

"What difference does it make?" Paige's smile flashed in a replica of the brunette's. "You know where to reach me—practically anytime." Then, reverting to her usual tones, "But don't call me, I'll call you. No wonder you were tired this morning! You'd had a busy night, working the clock around. Miss Barrett for the night shift, before you fitted me in this morning." She shook off his detaining hand with an angry gesture. "What do you do in the afternoons? Hunt for female lammergeyers?"

163

Alan's expression had gotten progressively stonier as her tirade continued. When she finally paused for breath, he said, "I don't have to. They're all over the place. Would you have preferred that I'd told her what we were really doing?"

She flushed under his derisive look, which showed he remembered exactly how enthusiastically she'd co-operated in that venture.

It was even more deflating when she realized that he'd merely been filling time—apparently while searching for a more permanent address at the beach. "You could have told me that you weren't happy with your living arrangement," she told him stiffly. "Nobody likes to hear things secondhand, especially from a stranger."

He ignored the last part of her criticism, concentrating instead on her main complaint. "What arrangement? I don't know what the devil you're talking about."

"You said she handled beach property."

"Oh, that! And you thought—" he broke off, clearly to avoid saying something he'd regret and then went on in a controlled tone, "I'm trying to find a place for George. At this point, he doesn't need a lab to check his work—just adequate office space. And maybe a beach house nearby for his living arrangements. There'll be some breathing time for him when we secure the government grant our company's after. I never planned to spend more than a week or two here. I have to get back to work."

Paige translated that to mean, "So don't get any wrong ideas." Like most men, he was setting out the ground rules early on—in case she'd misinterpreted his casual fling at lovemaking. Not that she was apt to, since he'd sandwiched it neatly between beach-combing and chatting up Barbara Barrett.

She balled her fists in her jacket pocket as she thought about it, so unhappy that her fingernails cut into her palms. There wasn't any way to win in her tangles with Alan. She'd been aware of that the first time she'd seen him and had been doing her best to keep her guard up ever since. Only she'd abandoned common sense during that last interval. Or was it the realization that she'd fallen head over heels for the man, so she'd let emotion and desire win for once?

But now it was all over and damned if she'd keep on playing the fool. After this, he could get Barbara Barrett or some other willing female to fall in his arms, but not his poor sap of a landlady.

The decision made her suddenly ache all over—an ache very different from the one she'd felt when Alan's strong body had been holding her captive in the sand. She bit hard on the edge of her lip to keep it from trembling, and took a deep breath. "If you'll excuse me," she said tonelessly, "I have work to do."

"Right. Don't let me keep you." Alan sounded just as terse as he turned on his heel, pausing only to swing the rucksack on his shoulders before he started down the beach in the same direction that the Barrett woman had taken moments before.

Paige didn't wait to see any more. She walked swiftly back up the path through the trees to the house. Once she'd unlocked the door, she paused only long enough to throw off her jacket before searching out Janet's unabridged dictionary and looking up Alan's damned lammergeyer, whatever it was.

It didn't help her morale to learn that it was an unattractive Eurasian vulture with talons and a malevolent expression. Suddenly she understood why Alan thought he was knee-deep in them around Cameron Cove, for as she surveyed her woebegone reflection in the mirror, there was a decided resemblance!

Chapter Seven

Paige wasn't able to indulge in her fit of the blues for long; the doorbell pealed imperiously as soon as she went toward the bathroom to wash the tears from her cheeks.

Alan! she thought with momentary panic. She certainly didn't want him to find her with red-rimmed eyes. Probably the best thing was to disregard his summons.

The doorbell sounded again, punctuated this time with a heavy knock on the front door. Paige grimaced and hurriedly dried her face, aware that he wasn't going to be ignored—even if it meant coming through her balcony window.

Another series of knocks brought her running down the hallway, her indignation rising with every step. She flung open the door, announcing angrily, "You didn't have to break it down—oh! I'm sorry!" The last came as she beheld Chief Sherwood's uniformed figure taking up most of the front porch. "I–I thought it was someone else," she apologized, feeling like an utter fool. "Won't you come in?"

"Not now, thanks. I'm trying to find Mr. Bayne. Do you know where he might be?"

"He was on the beach a little while ago—" Her voice broke as footsteps sounded on the path at the corner of the house. She managed a thin smile. "Speak of the devil—"

". . . and he's sure to appear," Alan said, coming into view. His austere expression changed abruptly as he recognized the policeman beside her. "Something wrong?"

"It's a missing persons report from Depoe Bay," the officer said. "A charter boat captain reports that two passengers disappeared this morning. George Porter and Liza Strom." The police chief cast a sympathetic look at Paige when she drew a shocked breath. "Liza gave your name and Mr. Bayne's as references when they hired the boat yesterday."

"When did he find out they were missing?" Alan asked, a perturbed look on his face. "I was talking to George just last night."

"Apparently it was first thing this morning," Chief Sherwood said, checking the clipboard he was carrying. "The two of them came aboard early. Shortly afterward, the captain went over to another dock to pick up bait for their outing, leaving them drinking coffee in the cabin. They'd disappeared when he came back a half-hour later. There was a blood stain on the side of the cabin door and another fishing boat captain reported seeing a woman struggling before she was put in a truck. The vehicle was some ordinary make and he can't even remember the color. Didn't think too much about it because at the time he figured it was a family fracas."

"Oh, Lord!" Paige exclaimed, half under her breath.

"And that's all you've got?" Alan asked, his voice tight.

"That's it. I take it you can't add anything to the report," the chief concluded, his glance intent.

"Not a thing. We've been on the beach"—Alan's gesture included Paige—"most of the morning."

"Okay. It made sense to check, and I couldn't raise you on the phone. I'm on my way to Depoe Bay now. We may turn up something."

"I'd like to go with you," Alan said. "Knowing both of them, I might be of some help."

He didn't mention identifying bodies, but since it was in all their minds, he might as well have, Paige thought. She came back to the present abruptly as Chief Sherwood nodded and told him, "Okay, but if you're going with me, it'll have to be right now. I can't waste any time."

"What about me?" Paige asked, as both of them turned toward the street. "Isn't there something I can do to help?"

Chief Sherwood spoke up first. "I shouldn't think so, Miss Kendall. Naturally, you'll be notified if there's any definite news. Will you be here?"

"I guess so," she replied, still upset by his disclosure. "Or maybe the office."

"Why don't you forget about work for a while?"

Alan asked. "There's nothing that won't wait until tomorrow."

She pushed a strand of hair back from her cheek distractedly. "I'll see. Anyhow, you'll be able to reach me either here or there," she told him. "And Alan, be careful."

The last words came out reluctantly, but she simply couldn't let him go off without showing him that she regretted their disagreement.

He nodded, watching the chief start toward his car before he added, "Don't worry too much. George isn't helpless, and if I ever saw a woman in charge of things, it's Liza. Five'll get you ten that they'll show up before we even reach Depoe Bay." He started toward the curb, adding over his shoulder, "I'll keep you posted."

She managed to smile and wave until the police car disappeared up toward the highway. Then she sagged back against the front door, wondering what else could go wrong in the hours to come. She knew that Alan had been only trying to keep up her morale with his assurances. Chief Sherwood hadn't handed out any snippets of cheer; if anything, his expression had more closely resembled that miserable Eurasian lammergeyer pictured in the dictionary. Paige scuffed a rhododendron leaf back into a shrubbery bed where it belonged and went into the house again.

She changed into a coral wool shirtwaist because its cheery color raised her morale and it was suitable for office wear. It was all very well for Alan to suggest that she take things easy, but he didn't realize how much Janet counted on the office income to augment her budget. And besides, Paige rationalized, she couldn't just sit around waiting for the phone to ring. At least in the office, she could dust the premises or do some filing in the meantime. She was too keyed up to face Alan's manuscript, and as far as his required reading went, she scooped up the stack of paperbacks and dumped them unceremoniously in a bureau drawer. She'd take them over to the annex when Alan returned and let *him* read the pithy parts. Not that he needed to; the episode on the beach had shown that he didn't require any instruction along that line.

The recollection made her mutter unhappily because she'd pushed that episode to the back of her mind on hearing the news of Liza and George's disappearance. Now, she could take her choice of dismal topics, it seemed.

She didn't waste any more time in the house, lingering only to put on her nylon raincoat and pick up her purse before letting herself out into the carport.

There weren't any neighbors in view as she backed into the street and, as a fine mist covered the car's windshield, she could understand why. Another rainy day at the beach!

The office took on a cozier note when she'd turned up the electric heat and plugged in the coffeepot. She hung her coat next to an old jacket of Liza's on the oak coat tree, and unconsciously ran her fingers down the front of it, as if the contact might help. "But that's dumb," she told herself fiercely afterward, "because Liza will be perfectly all right. Probably she'll be calling to complain about having to work over-time any minute now."

She felt better after that and went over to check the schedule which Janet had left atop the desk.

She'd noted that Liza had completed most of their regular weekly assignments when the phone rang, and she leaped for the receiver. Unfortunately, it was only a councilwoman calling to report that the regular meeting of the clam commission would be postponed until the chairman got over his cold, so there wouldn't be any notes to take for their records. She also wanted to hear about Janet's wedding and Paige was happy to tell her all she knew.

After she'd hung up, Paige poured herself a cup of coffee and stared out onto the street while she drank it, wondering how long it would be before she could expect to hear anything from Depoe Bay. She went back and sat in the swivel chair, swinging idly from side to side. Janet's carnelian agate paperweight, which had been a recent birthday gift from Seth, caught her attention then, and she picked up the graceful stone with its reddish undertones and smoothed her thumb over the glossy surface. She kept it balanced in one hand while turning to the dicta-phone recorder beside the typewriter. At least she could rewind the tape and have it ready for its next use.

The mechanism was simple and she'd just finished the rewind and was testing the next key when she heard the office door open. "Thor," she exclaimed, surprised to find him on the threshold. "How nice to see you! I could do with some company."

172

"You're not busy?" he asked, nodding toward the microphone in her hand.

She shook her head and clicked it off, replacing the paperweight in the same motion. "Just filling time. Have you heard the news?"

"You mean about the basketball team winning for a change?"

"No, I'm serious. It's George and Liza—they're missing."

His pleasant face stiffened with incredulity. "S'truth? Who told you that? I thought you said there wasn't any need to worry."

She rested her elbows on the desk and leaned disconsolately against her palms. "I know—but that was earlier. Chief Sherwood came by the house just a while ago to ask if we'd heard anything. He said they'd been kidnapped."

"My God!" Thor breathed. "Who'd do a thing like that?"

"I don't know." She rubbed her forehead with her fingertips as if trying to clear her thoughts. "We wouldn't have believed it except that the chief mentioned an eyewitness who'd seen Liza being forced in a truck."

"Who's 'we'?" Thor asked tersely, as if trying to sort things out.

She stared at him and then said, "Alan, of course. He was the one Chief Sherwood came to see."

"Ummm." Thor rubbed a thumbnail along his jaw, a preoccupied expression still on his face. "And where's Alan now?"

"He went with the chief to Depoe Bay. The authorities are trying to set up a command post or something. Alan thought he could help." She swallowed, as if the next words were hard to get out. "For identification, I think."

"Oh, for hell's sake—why are you writing those two off? You know Liza—nobody's going to hang onto her for long. Not if they have any choice."

"That's a terrible thing to say! Heaven knows what could have happened to her by now. There are lots of crazies attracted to the beach these days. You've told me so yourself!"

He picked up her coat and tossed it across the desk without ceremony. "Well, there's no point in sitting around here hanging crepe. Come on!"

She half-rose to her feet, staring at him dubiously. "Where are we going?"

"To Depoe Bay—if that's where the action is."

"But I—I—" Paige was going to say, "I wasn't invited," and then realized how absurd it would sound. Thor was right. There must be something helpful that they could do if they were on the scene. Maybe his cruiser could be pressed into service if the Coast Guard decided to search the rugged coastline. She straightened and reached for her raincoat. "You're right. Just give me a minute until I fix the answering machine."

He nodded and went toward the door. "I've got some perishables on the front seat of the car. I'll transfer them to the trunk for the time being. Don't drag your feet, love."

As the door slammed behind him, Paige quickly went over to unplug the percolator and turned the sign in the window to "Closed." She was just about to flip the key on the automatic answering device when the phone rang at her elbow.

Paige gasped, startled, and then grabbed the receiver. "Hullo?"

"Is that you, Paige?"

"Liza!" Paige's knees buckled at hearing the familiar voice, and she had to cling to the desk to stay upright. "Are you all right? No—where are you? That's the important thing."

"They're both important, believe me." The other tried for her usual antiseptic tone but Paige could hear an uncertain waver underneath the words. "I'm okay," Liza went on before she could comment on it. "Bruised around the edges, but I got away from the creep. Alan told me to let you know."

"That's wonderful! But where's George? Is he all right?"

What sounded like a sob came over the wire and then Liza said, "I hope so. The police think they know where he is and they're closing in. I should hear pretty soon. Oh, Paige—that damned fool hit him harder than he meant—" Her voice broke then as she started to cry.

"Listen, Liza, don't try to talk any more. Thor and I are on the way. We should be in Depoe Bay in about forty minutes."

"But Paige—"

"Just relax," Paige said, ignoring her protest. "There must be something we can do to help. I'll see you soon, dear."

Thor had the car door open as she flew down the

steps. "I was about to send up rockets," he began and then asked sharply, "What's happened? You look different."

"It's Liza," Paige interrupted as she dived into the front seat. "She's found! I mean, she just phoned and said she'd got away from the man. Isn't it wonderful! I thought we were going to go," she complained as he still stood beside the car, stupefied.

He roused himself with an effort. "We are," he said, sliding behind the wheel and slamming the door. "I was trying to sort things out. Is she in Depoe Bay?"

Paige looked blank, realizing that Liza hadn't mentioned locale. "She must be; she would have said if she weren't."

Thor shook his head as if her logic escaped him, but he switched on the ignition and reversed the sports car with his usual speed.

Paige clung to the edge of her bucket seat as he accelerated onto the highway. "I'd forgotten that you insist on flying low. Could we please arrive in one piece?"

"Have I ever delivered you any other way?"

"No, but it's so messy."

He took his attention from the highway long enough to shoot her a frowning look. "What do you mean by that?"

"It's just that you have my fingerprints over everything afterward—from clutching the edge of the seat and the dashboard."

"That's because you don't have faith in me. Relax and enjoy the scenery."

"I would, but it's whizzing by so fast that I can't see it."

He heaved a noisy sigh. "All right, all right. We'll go a little slower. I just thought you wanted to get down to Depoe Bay and hold Liza's hand as quick as possible."

"I do, but five minutes won't make any difference in the long run." She gave him a wistful smile. "Come on, Thor. Don't be stuffy now that we've heard such good news!"

"I wasn't mad about that—it's your back seat driving. No, don't say any more." He lifted his foot from the accelerator for a moment, lessening their speed. "We'll go down like a Sunday driver out admiring the countryside. And you'd damned well better look at the view now that you have the chance."

"Yes sir, I promise." She sat back then, glad that he'd decided not to sulk. For years, Thor had felt he possessed a budding talent as a race driver. The fact that he'd suffered minor mishaps in the only two competitions he'd entered did nothing to discourage him. The state highway patrol wasn't impressed by his efforts, either, and had ticketed him for speeding several times. Thor managed to hang onto his driving license despite the citations but was incensed if any of his friends mentioned them.

They maintained a truce for a few miles while Paige let her thoughts wander back to the telephone call, visualizing Liza's relief at finding herself free again. "Now if only George is all right," she murmured, thinking aloud.

"What's that?"

"I was going over what Liza said and crossing my fingers for George."

The car swerved lightly. "You mean, he wasn't with her?"

"Why, no—she was the only one who got away. I thought I'd told you." She shook her head apologetically. "Everything happened so fast."

"Well, sort yourself out and give me a blow-by-blow account," Thor said. "I gather they're still looking for him?"

"I guess so. Liza did say that the police think they know where he is. Hey!" The last came as he accelerated to pass a camper truck and had to swerve back to avoid an oncoming car.

Thor swore under his breath and then shot a sheepish glance her way. "Can't see three feet past one of those damned things! I hate to follow them." He edged out more carefully then and gave a murmur of satisfaction as he zipped around the older vehicle. "Now—what were you saying?"

Paige managed to hide her relief when he dropped his speed again. "I don't remember."

"About George. Where are they looking for him?"

Her eyes widened. "I haven't the foggiest notion. Oh, darn! I should have known better than to mention fog on this stretch of road." The last came when they hit a misty patch of weather as the highway curved over one of the scenic ocean views.

Thor's face took on a worried expression and he slowed even more as the mist on the road momentarily thickened. Then, it disappeared as quickly as before and the pale sun showed only a gently steaming highway in front of them.

Paige shook her head. "Ocean weather! It goes from A to Z and back again every day."

"It does at this time of year," Thor agreed. "I was just thinking—the weather might make it difficult."

"I don't follow you. . . ."

"If the police have to call in the Coast Guard. There's fog about now and storm warnings are due in early evening."

She half-turned to face him. "You think George might be aboard a boat? But their charter boat captain was the one who reported him missing in the first place."

"That isn't the only boat in Depoe Bay. Use your head, Paige," Thor said, sounding sorry that he'd brought the subject up.

She scowled back at his profile, unwilling to think of the possibilities. "I am—and I'll bet that he's safe and sound by now. Nobody's going to use a boat to kidnap a person. It would be like using a bicycle for the getaway from a bank robbery."

"You're probably right. But it would solve the problem of roadblocks," he pointed out stubbornly.

"Or getting rid of the body," she added before he could. "I've read detective stories, too, and the whole idea's ridiculous. Do you have anything to eat?"

He stared, taken by surprise. Then, when she inhaled sharply, he turned his attention back to the traffic. "Okay, I'll watch the road, but it's hard for me to keep up with you. There's a box of chocolate bars behind your seat. The coffee shop cashier put in a request for her display case when they left them off her latest order." As Paige leaned around to get one from the cache, he continued conversationally, "Besides, you're supposed to be looking at scenery, not thinking about food."

"Ummm." It was hard for Paige to say any more until she'd straightened again, triumphantly clutching a chocolate bar in her hand. She glanced out the car window then as the road climbed around another spectacular scenic viewpoint on the sheer hillside, where only a few coast pines managed to survive among the rock fissures. The trees were bent into bonsai shapes by years of onshore gales, adding a picturesque touch above the foaming ocean at the cliff's base.

Behind them, there was a timbered promontory where Douglas fir and western hemlock dwarfed their pine neighbors. Rampantly growing shrubs of chaparral broom and glossy Oregon grape shadowed their roots with thick undergrowths, providing a vista in variegated shades of green.

As Paige turned to the south again, the peninsula called Decatur Head came into sight. It was easy to identify because of its gleaming white lighthouse at the very edge, standing like a lonely sentinel in the picture postcard locale.

"It's a shame the Coast Guard abandoned Decatur Head," Paige told Thor, as she started to unwrap her candy bar. "All the tourists on the coast paid a visit to that light. Now, Janet says that the place is getting shabbier all the time."

"Nobody sees it. At least, the authorities tried to block off the road. Actually, it's still open because of that gravel pit just outside the federal property. The company's trucks have to get in and pick up their loads. Which gives me an idea," Thor said, swinging the car abruptly onto a graveled side road where a metal signpost saying "Decatur Head Lighthouse—Closed to Public" leaned at an awkward angle.

"What in the dickens!" Paige clutched at the chocolate bar as she lurched against the car door when Thor hit a pothole on the narrow track that wound up the side of Decatur Head. She turned her head to see the main highway disappear behind them as the side road curved again. "Why are we going here?" she asked Thor in some alarm.

"Don't get upset," he said, not bothering to slacken speed as the road straightened and they drove past the sprawling, old-fashioned office headquarters of Decatur Sand and Gravel Company. A man standing beside one of the big dump trucks stared after them, as Thor slowed slightly to avoid a warning sign which repeated that the road to Decatur Head lighthouse was officially closed.

"We're not supposed to be here," Paige said irritably, "and we *are* supposed to arrive at Depoe Bay. Liza will be expecting us."

"We'll be there," Thor said. "You get a view for miles from the lighthouse site."

"What does that have to do with it? We've already seen the view."

"I know," he said impatiently, "but I want to check the fog bank along the coast. I'm not volunteering my cruiser for any rescue operation if the weather's going to turn sour." He let up on the accelerator then as the road leveled. It was still hugging the cliffside, but the landscape had changed to clumps of broom and the spiny-leaved grape. "Look out there," he said, pointing over the magnificent expanse of ocean to the south. "Geese. They're migrating."

Despite her annoyance with his high-handed tactics, Paige peered through the windshield to admire the beautifully formed flock soaring overhead.

"Don't be mad, love," Thor coaxed, when she sat back again. "We won't be here long, and I have a lot of money tied up in that boat."

Paige felt like saying that there wasn't one chance in a hundred that the Coast Guard would commandeer a volunteer flotilla, but she could see there was no hope of changing Thor's mind just then. It would be better to let him check the weather and then urge him on to Depoe Bay, just a few miles down the highway. As Thor made a final turn to approach the old lighthouse, she could even look back through the low-hanging clouds and see the famous rocky harbor of the little fishing port.

Thor kept his attention straight ahead, driving up in the empty parking area and braking with a flourish. "Beautiful, isn't it?" he said, throwing out his hand in an expansive gesture that encompassed all the magnificent natural beauty around them.

Paige had to agree. Even the chipped paint on two

small outbuildings close by, which had once housed the lighthouse staff, couldn't spoil the greater overall beauty of seabirds nesting on the rocks just off the cliffside, the surf foaming along the miles of coastline, and the rugged grandeur of timbered hillsides. Even the lighthouse itself, though showing its age, stood with a quiet dignity, as if resting on its heritage and remembering the brave deeds of the men who'd served in it.

"Come on," Thor said, smiling as he started to get out of the car, "You can finish your candy bar in the fresh air."

Paige looked ruefully down at the melted chocolate in her palm. "I'm wearing most of it already and it'll be all over me in a minute. Do you have a napkin or something in the glove compartment? I must have left my handkerchief at home."

"For you, nothing but the best," Thor said, whipping a clean white handkerchief from his breast pocket.

"I hate to get that all chocolaty—" she said dubiously as she took it. "Oh well, I'll wash it for you afterward. Thanks so much."

She managed to clean the chocolate from her fingers after disposing of the rest of the bar in Thor's litter bag by her feet. Then, as a final touch, she blotted the edge of her lips in case she'd managed to smear the candy that far.

A faint scent of men's cologne wafted her way before she put the handkerchief down again. "Mmm— nice!" she said. "What is it?"

He remained motionless beside the still-open door,

staring intently at her. "Nothing special." Reaching for the handkerchief, he said, "Here, let me have it."

"No, I said I'd wash it. . . ."

As if in suspended animation, her voice slowed and then stopped as she recalled where she'd smelled that scent before. Realization rolled over her with the force of one of the breakers on the rocks far below. "The handkerchief—" she murmured painfully.

Thor swore violently under his breath.

She looked at him as if unable to believe her own conclusions, and hoping he'd deny them. "It was you that night in the annex. Your hand. Your handkerchief."

He didn't speak but the expression on his face told all she needed to know.

"Why, Thor?" Her voice was low and impassioned. "For God's sake, why?"

He shook his head as if words were beyond him and, shoving his hands in his pockets, stalked over to the edge of the cliff.

She watched him stand motionless, leaning carelessly against an off-limits sign which warned of dangerous ground and a protected seabird nesting area. After an instant, she got out of the car and went to join him. "Do you want to talk about it?"

He rounded on her forcefully. "What in the hell is there to say? That I needed money to keep the hotel going? That I couldn't let my father down? Would you understand that?"

Her features answered him even before she spoke. "There are lots of other ways. Why didn't you ask some of us for help? Good Lord, Thor!" She shook her head, as if unable to believe it still. "Housebreaking!"

"You didn't think I was looking for something to sell, did you?" he replied, stung. "I didn't rip off your television or the family silver." His anger showed in the rising tone of his voice. "There wasn't anything missing, was there? Not one damned toothpick! I wouldn't even have been there if it hadn't been for Alan Bayne and his pal, George."

"What did they have to do with it?" she faltered.

"Do you have any conceivable idea of how much that new process of George's is worth in industrial competition? I'm talking about other firms angling for millions of dollars in government grants to develop a similar formula."

Paige's eyebrows drew together as she looked up at his tense face. "You really mean industrial espionage, don't you? Cloak and dagger stuff here in Cameron Cove? You have to be kidding!"

"Get your mind out of the movies," he told her in an unflattering voice. "This isn't cloak and dagger—this is damned big bucks. People who came here to buy George's ideas and his process. Bayne wanted to get him out of reach until the government decision was made, but he didn't cover George's tracks very well. A couple of fellows checked into the hotel later the same night, and by then, I knew all about the situation."

"Thanks to a long session in the bar with George."

Thor smiled without any humor. "One up for you."

"But how did you know about the men?"

"Because they were willing to pay for a passkey to search his room."

Paige sagged against the other side of the signpost. "You didn't lose any time, did you?"

Thor's fair skin took on an unpleasant reddish tinge. "It's easy to have morals and principles with plenty of money in your pocket. These guys were businessmen wanting to deal. There was a commodity and they were willing to pay for it. I was glad to oblige."

"Even though it meant ransacking the annex?"

He shrugged. "We couldn't turn up anything of value in George's room. I told them there might be another angle. You should have been glad it was me. Those fellows play for keeps." Thor's glance went over her dispassionately. "If you'd interrupted one of them searching the annex, you might have come out of that closet in different shape."

Paige felt a shiver go down her body that had nothing to do with the penetrating dampness around them. A sudden guest of wind attacked two daffodils which still survived among the weeds, leveling them ruthlessly. Paige stared at the flowers, wondering if they'd outlive the next storm, and felt the first flicker of fear for her own survival.

Thor was going on, sounding aggrieved as he said, "I wish to hell you'd have stayed out of it. There was no reason for you to get involved."

"I didn't have a choice. All I did was take that manuscript back to the annex. I'm not even sure what we're doing here—unless all the rotten finagling didn't stop there." She couldn't hide her repugnance as her next words burst out. "Good Lord, Thor—I never thought you'd stoop low enough to be involved in a kidnapping!"

"I didn't plan anything like that in the beginning," he replied, his face a picture of misery. "But they wouldn't let me out. When I tried, they threatened to blow the whistle on me. Any bad publicity and my bankers would foreclose in a minute; it's only been luck that they haven't taken over before this. Anyway, I wasn't the one who abducted Liza and George. And they weren't to be hurt," he added virtuously.

As if he expected to be praised for not ordering their execution, Paige thought despairingly, aware for the first time how warped his reasoning had become. And nothing would be accomplished by haranguing him; all she could do was suggest that he turn himself in to the authorities and hope for leniency.

She bit her lip, wondering how best to approach the subject, and then froze as Thor grasped her arm in a steely grip. "You're hurting me . . ." she began, only to have him cut her off viciously.

"Quiet! Damn it all! Somebody's coming—how in the devil did they know?" His expression was thunderous as he stared down at her.

"Who? What are you talking about?"

"Can't you hear that engine?"

Paige strove to keep her balance as he shook her, aware that he was right; a car was coming up the lighthouse road at full throttle. Before she could think what it meant, Thor was hauling her back toward his car. She tried to hold back as he dragged her at his side. "Thor, don't be silly. You can't get away! Give yourself up—it'll be better in the long run!"

"The hell it will!" he gritted out when they reached the car, and he flung open the door.

"I'm *not* going with you!" she cried, struggling to escape his grasp. "You can't make me! You're out of your mind to try something like this!"

"Just stand there and shut up!" he ordered, with a warning jerk. Then, without wasting a minute, he slid into the driver's seat and closed the door, leaving her beside the car, gaping at him. "I need a little cover—"

"What are you going to do?"

"I've scheduled a private road race," he announced grimly, raising his voice as the noise of the approaching car cut through the quiet air. "All I need is two seconds' head start." He switched on his own ignition and gunned the motor, sparing her a sardonic grin in the process. "It's a good thing for you that I can go faster alone."

He stopped talking abruptly as a black and white patrol car burst around the last curve and, braking, careened sideways on the grass at the edge of the parking lot.

The moment's diversion was all Thor needed; he floored his own accelerator, fishtailing the car momentarily on the sandy dirt but managing to pull around the prowl car before the occupants could react. Paige didn't know what happened after that because the rear fender of Thor's car caught her as it slithered to gain traction, sending her sprawling in the weeds and dirt.

She heard a shot fired, shouts of masculine voices, and then Alan's familiar voice. He was beside her, saying anxiously, "Paige, darling! Are you all right? For God's sake, say something!"

Paige pulled herself up from the dirt and managed to give him a relieved and tremulous smile just before, in classic literary tradition, she passed out in his arms.

Chapter Eight

"I still say you were a damned fool for getting into the car with Thor in the first place."

Alan made his mild announcement as he and Paige sat in front of a cheery blaze in the annex fireplace late that afternoon. Since he punctuated the reproof with a light kiss on the end of her nose, Paige didn't take umbrage, settling even more comfortably against him on the couch.

"Not all of us come equipped with crystal balls," she said pertly. "Or minds like George's. Besides, I knew that Liza would remember what I'd told her on the phone—so there was hope."

"Yeah, but we wouldn't have come on like the cavalry if that man at the gravel company hadn't called to complain about somebody driving up their private road. As soon as he reported Thor's license number and the make of car to the police, we were able to . . ."

". . . cut us off at the pass. I watch westerns, too," she said, feathering a line across his cheek with her fingertip. "But I would have felt a lot happier if I'd known you were on the way. I had no idea that the police had rescued George by then, or arrested that creepy television repairman."

Alan captured her exploring finger, holding it firmly between his palms. "If you keep distracting me, we'll never get the explanations over with." His lips quirked in a grin. "Remember, I was all for going on to better things before this."

Paige tried very hard to appear severe but didn't succeed. Her outfit didn't help the illusion; she was wearing a medieval-styled taffeta blouse with deep ruffles for the collar, together with slim black velvet pants, and, with her hair loose and flowing, she looked more like a delectable sprite than a woman of substance. What was worse, she felt like it, and wasn't struggling to resurrect her other image.

"We still don't know the answers to a couple of things," Alan conceded as he reverted to more serious matters. "Apparently Thor got off Decatur Head by detouring on a dirt track. The police haven't caught up with him yet, but it's only a matter of time."

"He knows lots of people around here—I had the feeling he was going to try and hide out for a while."

"It occurred to me, too." Alan sighed as he got up to put another log on the fire. "Otherwise, he might have decided to take you along as a hostage. I know you're trying to give him the benefit of the doubt, but you didn't see the lump that George had collect-

191

ed—thanks to Thor's brilliant scheming. And it *was* his cruiser where we found George after that repairman knocked him unconscious."

"What about Liza?"

"Liza was the spanner in the works from the beginning. They didn't want her around but apparently didn't know what to do with her. So after the charter boat captain left to pick up their bait, your phony television repairman came aboard and knocked out George. Incidentally, what Thor didn't mention was that his chum was also a parolee who'd been out for hire in the past. Anyhow, by the time he'd taken care of George, who should appear from the forward cabin but Liza. Naturally, he wanted her out of the way—fast. He was seen shoving her in his panel truck, which was bad luck, but he managed to get her gagged and tied up, finally driving away. Since the one eyewitness thought it was a family fight, the alarm didn't go out then. That gave the repairman time to park on a back street and later transfer George onto Thor's cruiser."

"How did he manage that?"

"Simple. He'd moored the cruiser in an empty berth alongside the charter. George isn't a heavyweight, so all it took was a little muscle. Don't forget, it was barely daybreak, so he could count on getting George aboard the other cruiser unobserved. Then, all the repairman had to do was run the boat to the public pier and tie up again, pretending he was in for provisioning or bait or whatever."

"But why did he hang around? That seems awfully dangerous."

"Not really. Thor's cruiser was at Depoe Bay most of the time, so nobody gave it an extra glance. Besides, the man wasn't an expert sailor and he couldn't risk taking the cruiser through that tricky rocky gorge channel into the ocean, cracking up right in front of the Coast Guard. Apparently, Thor had been paid to handle the getaway and had arranged to moor the cruiser further down the coast. Then his backers were going to come aboard and 'persuade' George to change over to their side. Naturally, there's not a hell's chance of proving their complicity."

Alan dusted his hands after replacing the fireplace brush he'd been using to clean the hearth, and came back to the davenport, settling down with a satisfied sigh. "How's that for a blaze? I think I've missed my calling."

"If you can't finish that final chapter of your book, you may be looking for another occupation," Paige concurred, settling against his shoulder again. She half-turned to say severely, "But don't change the subject. What happened to finish off their scheme?"

"Liza's what happened. Apparently she spent a summer reading books on magic and illusions—including rope tricks. Damned if she didn't manage to escape from the truck. After that, she found the nearest phone and called the police to search Thor's cruiser. She thought its mooring alongside was too much of a coincidence, especially since it was supposed to be out on charter. After we took off to board it, she stopped to phone you."

"And I made her day by saying I was on the way with Thor."

"Lord, yes!" Alan looked almost gaunt as he rested his head against the back of the couch. "We'd found George but lost you. It was a bad time after that until the call came from that fellow who owns the gravel pit." There was a pause before he took a deep breath and hugged her even closer to him. "You're a terrible secretary, but I need you around."

"For that final chapter." As his head swooped to extract punishment, she ducked away—taking care not to get beyond arm's reach. "One more question."

"Make it fast," he commanded, a dangerous glint in his eyes.

"What's going to happen to George now? I mean, what's to keep him safe from trouble the next time?"

"Three things. First, the deadline for our government grant is only a couple days away. After that, George's services *and* his process are safely secured. Our competitors will have to search for new talent someplace else."

"But there are still two days."

"And George is fishing somewhere off the coast on a charter boat. There are two crewmen aboard and one's an off-duty deputy sheriff who happens to be an ex-wrestler."

Paige grinned but persisted. "You said three things. I can guess the last one. Liza."

"Who's worth her weight in gold. And the way she and George were cooing over each other when they left the dock, it's a good thing there were two chaperones aboard."

Paige pretended to consider it. "As a card-carrying expert in the field of love, I have to admit that there's something compelling about salt water and boats. Like a gravel beach or the heather or even a hearth rug."

The silence that followed her words came about as two pairs of eyes were directed slowly and inexorably toward the Navajo hearth rug in front of the fireplace.

"And that brings us finally to the really important part of this discussion," Alan said, meeting her glance. "I can hear the trap snapping shut on me, but I'd kill anybody who tried to open it." He continued whimsically, "I don't seem to have any choice. I haven't had since that first day when you handed out my high-button shoes."

"Rubbers," she corrected.

"Don't interrupt," he admonished, brushing his lips on the soft skin behind her ear. "I'm about to propose and I've never done it before, so God knows what will happen if you stop me in the middle." He noted the sudden moisture in her glance and shook his head. "I didn't know women cried when they received a marriage proposal."

Paige's voice was tremulous, but she managed to reply. "They only cry when they're going to say 'yes.'"

At her words, he caught her to him so tightly that she thought her ribs would break. So they break, Paige thought ecstatically, and wound her arms around his neck to get even closer as his lips covered hers.

She felt his hands moving possessively over her, awakening her desires and rousing her senses unmercifully on their exploring trail.

She had no idea how much time passed before Alan suddenly pushed away from her, breathing hard. "Dear heaven, you're not safe to be around. I knew that the first time you took a milk bath in those pajamas."

Paige's voice was as uneven as his. "You certainly didn't show it. I thought you were just planning to combine business with pleasure while you were here. You made me furious."

"I know," he said wryly.

"But only because I wanted to say yes—and I'd never felt that way before."

"You weren't the only one. I was completely off balance, too. I told myself the only safe thing was to keep as far away from you as possible."

"Leaving me with that darned required reading." She tilted her head to look at him. "That was another scam, wasn't it? You didn't need that material."

He started to chuckle at her stern look. "If you could have seen your face when I mentioned sex research that first time! Ouch! You bit me!" he accused, prying her away from his shoulder.

"I'd like to do more than that, you beast!"

"Mmmm." He brought her back against him so fast that she felt like a rag doll, draped across his chest. "So would I," he murmured against her willing lips, "and I sure as hell intend to. The question is, when?"

She pushed back to give him an incredulous look. "You need a schedule for it?"

"Don't be a fool! Listen to me, woman. Somehow in the next week we have to fit in getting married, the last chapter of my book, taking care of your sister's business, retrieving Jonah from the vet, and baby-sitting the house—not necessarily in that order. Am I right?"

She placed a soft kiss in the palm of his hand and closed his fingers over it. "Send my compliments along—you're doing fine."

He gave her a rueful, half-angry glance. "You don't make it easy on a guy."

"Sorry."

"And don't look at me that way. What I'm letting myself in for!" He burrowed his lips in her hair for a brief, devastating moment.

"I'll behave," she promised, and started to laugh at his suddenly stricken look. "Within reason. Tell me, what do we do first?"

"Well, I don't know about you, but I'd never survive a long engagement. How about a charter flight to Nevada, coming back here afterward for a honeymoon?"

"It sounds heavenly. We can hunt for agates and go bird-watching again—concentrating on lammergeyers."

"And you can tell me more about what you've learned in your reading," he said solemnly. "It might come in handy one of these days or nights."

She stared at him, wide-eyed. "For your writing?"

"Naturally." His voice deepened. "An author has

to be sure of his facts. We could maybe try out the gravel beach in our spare time—there are lots of those around here."

"And a patch of heather up on the hill, too."

"That only leaves the hearth rug." Alan's eyes were alight with laughter as he held her gaze. Then his expression took on a more thoughtful look as he put her away from him and stood up to check the screen on the fire.

Paige watched him carefully, sensing disquiet in his sudden retreat.

Alan didn't leave her wondering long. He cleared his throat, sounding almost embarrassed as he said, "I'm not against heather or beaches"—he smiled crookedly—"or even milk baths. They can add plenty of excitement to making love. Nobody needs to read a book to know that. But this afternoon—when I heard you were missing—and afterward when I didn't know what we'd find up on Decatur Head, I learned about another kind of love. The kind that doesn't need any folderol to make it last. Of course, I might be out shopping for ground-up rhino horn or a dozen oysters when we're celebrating our sixtieth anniversary," he said, his eyes gleaming wickedly again. "In the meantime, I know enough to stay off hearth rugs while you're nearby." He detoured past the one by the fireplace as he came back to pull Paige up in his arms. "Playing around on one of those means we'd sure as hell be looking for a minister in Nevada tomorrow morning instead of tonight."

Paige wished there were some way to say that she couldn't love him any more than she did at that very

198

moment. Fortunately, her shining, tear-drenched eyes were more eloquent than she knew, because Alan dropped a quick kiss on her wet cheek and pulled her determinedly toward the front door.

"Remind me to tell you about a new sex gimmick while we're on the way to the airport," he said conversationally. "It's called a double bed. People say it won't last, but if there's one at the hotel in Nevada—we might as well give it a try."

About the Author

Glenna Finley is a native of Washington State. She earned her degree from Stanford University in Russian Studies and in Speech and Dramatic Arts, with emphasis on radio.

After a stint in radio and publicity work in Seattle, she went to New York City to work for NBC as a producer in its international division. In addition, she worked with the "March of Time" and *Life* magazine.

As a producer, she had her own show about activities in Manhattan, a show that was broadcast to England. The programs were similar to those of the "Voice of America."

Though her life in New York was exciting, she eventually returned to the Northwest where she married. Currently residing in Seattle with her husband, Donald Witte, and their son, she loves to travel, and draws heavily on her travels and experiences for the novels that have been published. Her books for NAL have sold several million copies.

The Best Romance Fiction from SIGNET